By Charles Bukowski
Available from Ecco

The Days Run Away Like Wild Horses Over the Hills (1969)

Post Office (1971)

Mockingbird Wish Me Luck (1972)

South of No North (1973)

Burning in Water, Drowning in Flame: Selected Poems 1955–1973 (1974)

Factotum (1975)

Love Is a Dog from Hell: Poems 1974–1977 (1977)

Women (1978)

You Kissed Lily (1978)

Play the piano drunk Like a percussion Instrument Until the fingers begin to bleed a bit (1979)

Shakespeare Never Did This (1979)

Dangling in the Tournefortia (1981)

Ham on Rye (1982)

Bring Me Your Love (1983)

Hot Water Music (1983)

There's No Business (1984)

War All the Time: Poems 1981–1984 (1984)

You Get So Alone at Times That It Just Makes Sense (1986)

The Movie: "Barfly" (1987)

The Roominghouse Madrigals: Early Selected Poems 1946–1966 (1988)

Hollywood (1989)

Septuagenarian Stew: Stories & Poems (1990)

The Last Night of the Earth Poems (1992)

Screams from the Balcony: Selected Letters 1960–1970 (1993)

Pulp (1994)

Living on Luck: Selected Letters 1960s–1970s (Volume 2) (1995)

Betting on the Muse: Poems & Stories (1996)

Bone Palace Ballet: New Poems (1997)

The Captain Is Out to Lunch and the Sailors Have Taken Over the Ship (1998)

Reach for the Sun: Selected Letters 1978–1994 (Volume 3) (1999)

What Matters Most Is How Well You Walk Through the Fire: New Poems (1999)

Open All Night: New Poems (2000)

Beerspit Night and Cursing: The Correspondence of Charles Bukowski & Sheri Martinelli 1960–1967 (2001)

The Night Torn Mad with Footsteps: New Poems (2001)

sifting through the madness for the Word, the line, the way: new poems (2002)

CHARLES BUKOWSKI

OPEN ALL NIGHT
NEW POEMS

ecco

An Imprint of HarperCollinsPublishers

HarperCollins books may be purchased for educational, business, or sales promotional use. For information, please e-mail the Special Markets Department at SPsales@harpercollins.com.

ACKNOWLEDGMENTS

These poems, written between 1970 and 1990, are part of an archive that Charles Bukowski left to be published after his death. On behalf of the author, the publisher would like to thank the editors of the periodicals where some of these poems first appeared.

First Ecco edition published in 2003.

LIBRARY OF CONGRESS CATALOGING-IN-PUBLICATION DATA

Bukowski, Charles, 1920–1994.
   Open all night : new poems / Charles Bukowski.
     p. cm.
   ISBN 1-57423-135-9 (paperback)
   ISBN 1-57423-136-7 (cloth trade)
   ISBN 1-57423-137-5 (deluxe cloth)
    I. Title
  PS3552.U4 O6   2000
   811'.54—dc21   00-60833

HB 08.16.2022

For
Nikhil Henry Bukowski Sahoo

Table of Contents

2. FLIGHT TIME TO NOWHERE

4. LAZY IN SAN PEDRO

OPEN ALL NIGHT
NEW POEMS

1

hymn from the hurricane

2 buddies

I am not sure of our exact ages
when we met
(perhaps 9 or 10)
but Moses was one of my first real
friends:
Jewish and very quiet
and my second real friend was
Red—
he had one healthy arm
and part of another:
the lower part of his right
arm was a pure white enamel with a
brown leather glove
over the artificial fingers.

Moses vanished first.
my father informed me about him:
he pointed to a garage down the street
a large white and yellow structure
with sagging doors:
"your friend Moses was caught in *there*
doing something to a 5-year-old
girl. they got him."

Red's friendship was more durable.
we went swimming together all summer in the public
pool. he had to remove his artificial arm
as he splashed about with his arm-and-a-
half, the short arm ending just below
the elbow. it looked like it had
tiny nipples on the end of it
or maybe
it looked like tiny fingers.

the other boys teased him about his
half-arm and his tiny fingers
but I was a very mean lad
and I told them
in terms most definite

that the pool belonged to
everybody
and to let him
swim
god-damn-it
or else.

sometimes this brought us trouble later:
a gang would follow us home
to his house or mine and
more than once
standing outside
they'd scream at us
until we came out
and met them on the front
lawn.

I wasn't as good as Red.
he was very good with his pure white arm
with the brown glove,
it was usually around 4 or 5
against 2
but Red simply clubbed them down
one after another
swinging that hard arm
I'd hear the sound of it against
skulls
and there would be boys down on the lawn
holding their heads
and this only made me meaner
and I'd get one or two of my
own
and soon everybody but Red and
myself would have vanished off the
street.

we went swimming in the public pool
together
more and more often.
there always seemed to be new boys
always more new boys

who couldn't quite grasp
how it worked.
they just didn't understand that we only
wanted to swim and be left
alone.

harking back to
Moses
I'm not so sure
but in a way
unfortunately
he must have been
missing some parts
too.
we never saw him again
but his mother sure could
cook
I remember all those delicious
cooking smells throughout the
house.

I never saw Red's mother cooking
anything.

Saturday afternoon

we must have been 14 or 15
and we sat in this movie house
and here came this blonde on the screen
with pale empty eyes
and my friend elbowed me and said,
"Jesus, Hank, look at her *lips!*
look how *moist* those lips are!
I want to kiss those *lips!*"

"Jesus, man," I said, "shut
up!"

all the guys around us could hear
him.

"I'm in *love!*" he said.

"God damn," I said, "shut up
or I'll punch you!"

I didn't like blondes: their skin
was like ivory and they always
looked like they were about to
faint.

"it's her *lips,*" he said, "oh,
shit, it's those *lips!* look at
them! just to kiss those
lips!"

the blonde was falling into some
man's arms like a swooning
butterfly and it was Gable,
my man Gable was falling for it!
it wasn't a good afternoon.

"I'd cut off one of my balls
just to *kiss* her!" my friend
said.

"shit," I said and got up and
walked out.
I didn't want to hang around an
asshole like that.

I walked down to Frenchy's Café
for a coke.
I got the coke and sat there
and lit a cigarette.

"you can't smoke in here,"
said Frenchy, "you're just a
kid."

I kept smoking—I knew I
could handle Frenchy: he'd
been eating his own food, mostly
hot dogs and fries, for years and he
weighed about three hundred and
eleven pounds.

"so, you think you're a man,
huh?" he asked.

I nodded in the
affirmative.

"o.k., how'd you like to try
Stella?"

I shrugged.
Stella was Frenchy's waitress.
she walked out with her enormous
hips and her large yellow
teeth.

"Stella, the kid says he wants to
hide it in your doughnut!"

"oh yeah?" she smiled at me.

she scribbled something down
on a pad, ripped off the page
and handed it to me.

"that's where I live. bring $5 and come
by after seven..."

then she walked back
into the kitchen where she
washed dishes during slow
times.

Frenchy leaned across the
counter and grinned at me,
"you think you can handle her,
kid?"

I drained the coke,
gave him his money,
said, "better than *your*
fat ass could, Frog..."

then I walked back down
the hill to my house
and my mother asked,
"back from the movie already,
Henry?"

"yeah," I said and I walked
into the bedroom
closed the door and stretched
out on the bed
knowing that I was afraid of
Stella and that I was afraid of
the blonde in the movie and
that I really didn't want
either one of them.

then the door opened and
my mother stood there
and she said, "Henry,

what are you doing in bed
at three-thirty on a Saturday
afternoon?
it's not good for young boys
to be laying around
and not doing anything!
young boys should be *doing*
something!"

I got up and walked out of
the bedroom and out of the
house and I began walking
down the street and I
turned the corner at twenty-
first street and I walked
down twenty-first street
and I kept walking and
walking past
hedges and driveways and
houses, and there
were men mowing and watering
their lawns, and there were
dogs barking, and there was
nothing else to do, there was
absolutely nothing else for me to
do.

young love

we were nineteen,
Angel, the little dark guy,
Robert, the stubby muscled guy and
me, of the sunken cheeks and belly.
we lived in tiny rooms and
each meal was
a miracle and
the week's rent
more so
and one Sunday we
decided to go to a movie
which was a crazy
luxury—
none of us had seen a movie since
our parents had
kicked us out.

"which one?" asked Robert.
"I don't care," I said, "they're all
equally bad."

but
Angel was in love with a
rather fat actress with big
eyes, eyes always
filled with tears, so
we drove down Pico Blvd.
in a car
Robert had borrowed from
his older brother
and we found the theatre
with Angel's actress and
we paid and
went in
and her movie was
on first—
it had to do
with bastards (the real kind)
and since our parents had

treated us as such
in the past
we paid some interest
although
we mainly liked the lady's
weeping eyes and big
thighs: I'm sure we
all imagined ourselves
in bed with her
getting healed.

in her best scene
she said furiously,
"there is no
such *thing* as *illegitimate*
children! there are only
illegitimate parents!"

the second movie was about
Love in the South
during
old plantation days.
it was just before the
Civil War
and
most of the gentlemen were
gentlemen and most of the
ladies were still ladies.
it was a musical
and the plot was confusing:
there seemed to be some
problems brewing but they
were so subtle that
I couldn't quite grasp what
they were.

anyhow, a scene arrived
where the
two lovers (him and her)
went out on a
balcony

and began singing a
love duet to
one another.

"now," I told Robert, "if
the slaves come in from the
fields and start singing with
the lovers
I'm leaving."

it didn't take long.
the blacks came in, yes, a
black sea of them, soon over a
hundred faces, maybe two hundred,
male and female
young, medium, very old, even
some tiny children
looking up at the balcony
and singing to the two lovers as
the two lovers sang
to each other.

"let's go," said Robert.

"o.k.," I said.

"hey," said Angel, "where the hell are
you guys going?"

"we'll wait for you in the car,"
Robert told him.

Robert and I pooled our money and
bought a large loaf of French bread
and sat in the car
eating it.
it was fresh and very good
it filled the empty places.
when you're hungry and broke
one of the best things you can do

is fill up on French bread.
as we ate the French bread
we didn't talk very much
just now and then we
laughed
as we chewed.

soon we were finished.

not much later
Angel came out.
he got into the car:
"hey, you guys are *crazy!* you
wasted your *money!* you only got
to see *one* movie!"

Robert started the car and
we drove back down Pico Blvd. as the
sun was going down on
Los Angeles.

Angel was in the back
seat.

"you guys are crazy," he
said again.

somehow I don't think we were.

lioness

look, the lioness is hungry.
she stalks the wildebeest.
they are faster
but she is stronger
she can run longer.
and she is hungry.

there she goes,
bounding.
look, she almost has a young
wildebeest near the
rear of the pack.

yes, leap, she has him.
by the throat.
his eyes like bottlecaps
pray to the sky.

he's dead now
she tears him apart
going for her favorite
bits.
the others—
the birds and hyenas
close in and
wait.

she shakes her head
rises
slowly walks off.
as the monkeys begin to
come down out of the
trees
the lioness is
satisfied and
full.

dinner, pain & transport

slowly going
the way of witches,
banal and burning
having
dinners in cafés
where trolleycars run over
the roof, and
notes from the mayor
asking me to kill pale young
boys
who ride bicycles;
it is an indecent time
when the machine guns are silent
and the clouds hold nothing hidden
in creampuff jowls;
I can prophesy evil
with the force of a jackhammer
dislodging a stupid street;
I wipe my mouth and count the
bannister bars, I contemplate the
white space
between the waiter's legs
as he runs to hand me
a bill; outside,
it is the same:
the devils drink from the breasts
of stunned maids;
it is beginning to rain:
fleck, fleck, fleck,
the dirty drops of tulip wine...
I buy a paper at the corner,
fold it like a sleeping cobra
and stand there
stand there
drawing pictures in the air,
dirty pictures and cathedrals,
scalped lizards, drunken miracles;
then catch the 6:15 bus
to my room; it is a room

that catches dusty flies and
glass and paper, catches me,
and I will sleep there
to awaken to the intern's hand
through sick light, or it will be
the red taste of fire, smoke singing
like these birds in my walls.

love for the first whore

anti-woman, of course I was, and it's too
bad we must
preface this with that,
but now having wasted those incorrect words in this
enlightened year, let's get down to it, I was
ugly but tough, say 25 years old, I drank
heavily, probably screwed up with
self-pity but nevertheless had left a
few bloody lips and blackened eyes
along the way on the
dumb bulls who hung about those cheap
bars.
the girls liked this, but hell, you could hardly
call them
girls ...
anyhow, being a stock clerk or an unemployed
warehouseman
I was left the error of my ways and nights which I pissed
away in cheap bars,
got a rep as a tough drinker and a guy who
would say anything and was willing to
back that up.
you bored yet?
anyhow, in one of those bars was
Julia.
Julia of the GREAT legs
who never said anything
just sat there
drinking them down
head bowed,
large wart on left hand,
dropping her cigarette ashes everywhere,
then,
now and then
raising her head and pronouncing
in a profound way
(it seemed to me, anyhow)
the word
"SHIT!"

it splashed upon the walls and mirrors and on
me and I thought, looking at those
great legs, I would really like to
know this woman.

there didn't seem to be any barriers so
I sat down next to her and we drank
together and at closing time
we left for my hotel room
together.

getting bored?
well, I wasn't.

except getting her through the
hotel lobby was quite a trick—
those great legs on that great
body—she was wobbling on
high-heeled
shoes. (of course, this is
sexist—forgive me)
and I got her into the
elevator and up to my
room
where I plopped her down and
began pouring drinks ...
boring and standard, you
say?—not so.
I plopped her down in a chair
and she just smoked and
gulped down the
drinks.

but I didn't want a simple
copulation
I wanted to exhibit my
qualities.
I felt that I had big arms,
muscles, you know,
and powerful legs
which I had somehow

been born with
and I also felt that I had
interesting and
unusual things to say,
so I walked up and down
in my shorts
gulping down drinks,
pouring drinks,
burning holes in my
undershirt with hot
cigarette ashes
but she just continued to
look
indifferent
so I started smashing
glasses of wine
against the walls
and singing nationalist
socialist songs.

that awakened her a bit
and also the desk
clerk
who I told to
go frig himself
before I hung
up.

by the time the police
arrived
I was in full bore
under a full moon
between those great
legs.
the door was bolted
and the universe
sang my
song.

I lived with that whore
off and on

for 5 years
and such hell
you could never
imagine

unless you
were me
which we all have been
at one time or another
less or
more.

good times

I had been sad and hungover
for several days
and nights.
it was about 5 p.m.
I was in my shorts
spread across the
bed

puking into a
dishpan
looking down at
the
green-yellow
parts of taco
parts of me

after nights and days of
vodka, gin, beer, wine,
whiskey,
depression.

the door opened and there
was Jane.
she'd been gone two or three
days.

"just leave before I throw
you through the wall," I told
her.

"now, don't get *nasty*," she
said "Jerri scored and she's
proud as all get-out. she's got
her own room and a fifty-buck
bill and the guy left her a fifth
of scotch."

"o.k.," I said, "let's go ..."

I got off the bed, repaired to
the bathroom and got myself
together.

.

at Jerri's place she had her
radio on to loud cowboy music
as she sat on her bed
flipping through pages of
LIFE.

"hello, Jerri," Jane said.

"hello, Jerri," I said.

"hi!" she said. "I never got 50 bucks for
it before! the guy was a
millionaire!"

Jerri just smiled all over the
room.

Jane found some paper cups and
began pouring us some
refreshment.

"he was an angel," Jerri said.
"he sent his chauffeur into the bar
and the chauffeur drove me to
his mansion
and all I had to do was to
suck-off
his wife
while the millionaire watched
and the chauffeur took some
photos. that's all there was
to it."

"you mean—his wife?" I asked.

"yeah," she said, "she was
a big fat pig."

"this is *great* whiskey," Jane
said.

"let's have some more," I
suggested.

we did.
we sat there drinking the whiskey out
of paper cups,
Jerri on the bed, smiling,
Jane propped in a chair with her legs
on the bed and I was just rather
sitting in a chair.

"besides the $50," Jerri said, "they
got me this place and gave me the
fifth."

she just kept smiling across the
room
everywhere—
sometimes at us
sometimes at the walls
sometimes even
at the ceiling.

the year was 1953 and she was
very proud.

Jane and Prince

we all lived together
in a small shack in
central L.A.

there was a woman in bed
with me then

and there was a very large
dog
on the foot of the bed

and as they slept
I listened to them
breathe

and I thought, they depend
on me.
how very curious.

I still had that thought
in the morning
after our breakfast
while backing the car
out of the drive

the woman and the dog
on the front step
sitting and watching
me

as I laughed and waved
and as she smiled and
waved

and the dog watched
as I backed out into the
street and disappeared
into the city.

now tonight
many years later
I still think of them
sitting there on that
front step

it's like an old
movie—50 years
old—that nobody ever
saw or could understand
but me

and even though some
critics would dub this
ordinary

I like it
very much.

a place to hang out

to be young, foolish, poor and ugly
doesn't help to make life look any better.
so many evenings, examining the walls alone
with
nothing to smoke
nothing to eat
(we usually drank up my paycheck fast).
she always seemed eager to leave
eager to move on
but first she would
put me through her college—
(handing me my Masters and my Ph.D.
in the process)
and she always finally returned,
she wanted a place to hang out,
she said,
somewhere to keep her clothes.
she claimed I was funny,
that I made her laugh
but I was not trying to be
funny.
she had beautiful legs and she was
intelligent but she just didn't care
about anything,
and all my fury and my humor and
all my madness only entertained
her mildly: I was performing for her
like a sad puppet in some farce of my own.
a few times after she left I had enough
cheap wine and enough cigarettes on hand
for a few days,
I'd listen to the radio and look at the
walls and get drunk enough to
almost forget her
but then she would return once
again.
no other woman has made me feel as
low as I felt then
as on those evenings

during that two-mile hike home from work
turning up the alley
looking up at the window
and finding the shade dark.
she taught me then the agony of the damned and
the useless.
one wants a good woman, good luck, good
weather, good friends but
for me she was a long shot and
the time was cold and the longshot didn't
come in.
I buried her five winters after I met her,
seldom seeing her during the last three years.
there were only four of us at her grave:
the priest
her landlady
her son and myself.
it didn't matter as
I remembered
all those walks up the alley looking
in vain for a light behind the shade and as
I remembered
the dozens of men who had fucked her and
who were not there at the end.
yes, only
one of the men who had loved her
was there: "my crazy stockroom boy from the
department store," she called me.

to Jane Cooney Baker, died 1-22-62

and so you have gone
leaving me here
in a room with a torn shade
and *Siegfried's Idyll* playing on a small red radio.

and you left so quickly
as suddenly as you had arrived
and as I wiped your face and lips
you opened the largest eyes I have yet to see
and said, "I might have known
it would be you,"
and you did recognize me
but not for long
and an old man of white thin legs
in the next bed
said, "I don't want to die,"
and your blood came again
and I held it in the pail of my hands,
all that was left
of the nights, and the days too,
and the old man was still alive
but you were not
we are not.

and you went as you arrived,
you left me quickly,
you had left me so many times before
when I thought it would destroy me
but it did not
and you always returned.

now I have turned off the red radio
and somebody in the next apartment slams a door.
the indictment is final: I will not find you on the street
nor will the phone ring, and each moment will not
let me be in peace.

it is not enough that there are many deaths
and that this is not the first;

it is not enough that I may live many more days,
even perhaps, more years.

it is not enough.
the phone is like a dead animal that will
not speak. and when it speaks again it will
always be the wrong voice now.

I have waited before and you have always walked in through
the door. now you must wait for me.

I was her lover

it's my turn now
up through the green wave
blood bubbles,
my body
flesh on some great hook;
names, cities, dreams,
it's my turn now,
I have watched them all go,
friends and lovers,
I have watched the pianist play on
after the audience has left,
it's my turn to go now,
all large growing fit to a thimble,
down,
down
with them, with her,
cities taken and buried
this way,
animals like mountains
and mountains themselves,
lightning and prayer and then
the sea,
snuffed out we are
like nothing,
like nothing we are
and the pianist plays on
as small devils slide down the balustrade,
I am going
down now through the green wave
where no lightning can reach
hold me
air and water,
hold me,
blot out the
voices from faces that eat stale bread and grit
and speak nothing but lies,
I was her lover and she was life
and she turned her back and walked away.

beauty gone

you were, at best
the delicate thought of a delicate hand
and when
beneath the love of flowers I am still and gone—
as the spider drinks the greening hour—
strike grey bells,
let a frog say
                a voice is dead;
let the beasts of the forest,
the days that have hated this,
the contrary wives of unblinking grief
plan a small surrender somewhere
between Mexicali and Tampa;
you gone, cigarettes smoked, loaves sliced,
and lest this be taken for wry sorrow:
put the spider in wine,
crack the thin skull that held poor lightning,
make it all less than a treacherous kiss,
and put me down for the last dance
you much more dead than I:
I am a dish for your ashes,
I am a fist for your air.

the most immense thing about beauty
is finding it gone.

dogfight over L.A.

left wing down, I go after Mosk.
I have him in my sights, press the trigger.
he slides away at the last moment
as I trace a wavy line of bullet holes
just below the cockpit
and down into his tailfin.

my gunfire disfigures the words painted
on the side of his fuselage:
POETRY IS LOVE.

•

I first met him when I was living with
Loretta and Loretta was crazy and in love with
poetry and she sat at the feet of this
guy Mosk who taught a creative writing
class at the Unitarian church at 7th and
Vermont.

I was working a 12-hour nightshift while he
was sitting around with girls in pink
and yellow dresses
reading them his rhymes.

I got rid of Loretta but I kept running
into Mosk
at Van Gogh exhibitions, wine tastings and
garage sales.

he always looked the same: the
3 long hairs hanging from his chin;
his superior elfin grin
as he flashed his
A.C.L.U. membership card at
us;
and
he was one of those who
carried around a handful of sunflower

seeds, nibbling at them, it made
the ladies hot.

over Burbank I hammered off the tip of his
left wing
as he did a bellyroll. I straightened up,
dipped left over the L.A. Zoo frightening
the helpless boa constrictors, pelicans and alli-
gators.

Mosk was always involved with some
superior cause. he was
head of the Hydrogen Peroxide Play Group
which performed the same Brecht plays
over and over
again.
he was president of the Pasadena
Vegetarians
and he founded the
KILL HATE GROUP
which helped alcoholics and dope
fiends.
later
I met some of his patients; they looked very
unhappy.
(if you want to help an alcoholic you
give him a drink
and if you want to help a junkie you
give him a fix.
that asshole Mosk
had it all backwards).

once at a poetry reading
he told me, "you are a confused
man, probably the victim of an unhappy
childhood."

I grabbed him by the collar, "listen,
buddy, how would you like to eat a

bowl of my shit?"

"peace," he said, "I'm a pacifist."

"weighing 112 pounds and not having any
guts," I informed him, "you don't have
much choice."

I slammed him up against the wall and
walked out
leaving behind the manuscript of my unfinished
novel.

over East L.A. I gave him another burst
of machinegun fire
but I could see from the tracers that
I had missed his god-damned skull
by 3 feet.

you know, each man has one special
enemy, sometimes more than one.
I remember when I was a kid in grammar
school, every time I looked at Stanley Sherman
a flash of red would fire up
my eyes.
I'd feel like breaking his pencils
or dropping itch powder down the back of his
neck.
everybody else seemed to like him.
"what about this Stanley Sherman?"
I'd ask.
"shall we kill him?"
"oh, he's nice," they'd say.
"uh huh," I'd say ...

I don't know why the girls liked
Stanley. they stood around and admired him
while he glowed like a sunflower
after the rain.

I don't think he even had a dick. I think
he pissed out of his elbows.
but you know how girls are
they like guys in pants without wrinkles
in clean shirts and expensive sweaters
they like guys in shiny shoes who
say nice things to their mothers,
who keep that prissy smile working
day and night like a
neon sign advertising an empty motel
room.

oh yeah ... and those guys are always
carrying around a *book*.
isn't that something?

the girls must think those guys have
brains just because they get along
with everybody—the teachers, the P.T.A.
mothers and the crossing guards.
they don't realize that guys like that,
after decades of fake smiles,
fly apart like a
hand grenade
and in their mid-forties they
cut the heads off little girls and
stuff the remainder into garbage cans.

most people I can deal with.
I mean, I don't want to look at them or
listen to them, and I don't want them to
write or telephone, but I can deal
with them so long as they stay in their
space and let me have mine.
but with Stanley it was completely
off the board, it was the Hallelujah Chorus
played backwards with
Charles Manson conducting.

over Pomona, I got Mosk in my sights
again and I riddled the other side of
his fuselage
where he had painted:
IF YOU CAN'T LOVE, LEAVE.

next time around I'd have
him!

then my engine started sputtering.
I checked the gas gauge:
zero.

then I saw Mosk behind me.
he had me in his
sights.

it was over.

he was right on my tail, I could
see his ever-pleasant face, that
sunflower smile.

I was finished.

I turned and gave him the
finger.
I could see him smiling, and
chewing on his seeds.

I waited.

then he gave me the
peace sign and
swung off to the right
disappearing into a billowy
white cloud.

I nursed it down
looking for a place to land,
saw the Pomona racetrack,

a half-miler,
I'd been there hundreds of
times,
I went for the early
speed.

luckily, the season was over
and I brought it down
just where they turn into the home
stretch
bounced it down o.k. and
rolled it to a stop in front of
the winner's circle.

I climbed out, kicked the wheel,
then pissed on it.

shit.

next time I'd get him!
I'd blow his asshole out through his
bellybutton!

I walked toward the empty grandstand,
the dead toteboard at my
back.

Mosk, your mother eats raccoon
brains, and the smell of your world is
worse than rotten liver stinking in an
Algerian alley.

and yes, Mosk, your time is up.
when you have a man in your
sights and then you let him go
you don't have more than
two or three Tuesdays left to
kiss the sweet lips of this dirty
world
goodbye.

event

earlier tonight
there was a fire in the
neighborhood.
we stood there
watching the fire,
and when they put it out
there was nothing but the smell
of smoke and wet burned wood,
and then the firemen left
and we all went back
to our small rooms.
looking out the window
I could see 2 or 3
old women
in shawls
still talking about
it.
I walked to the stove
and put some coffee
on the burner and then
turned on the radio
for something
new.

all that

the only things I remember about
New York City
in the summer
are the fire escapes
and how the people go
out on the fire escapes
in the evening
when the sun is setting
on the other side
of the buildings
and some stretch out
and sleep there
while others sit quietly
where it's cool.

and on many
of the window sills
sit pots of geraniums or
planters filled with red
geraniums
and the
half-dressed people
rest there
on the fire escapes
and there are
red geraniums
everywhere.

this is really
something to see rather
than to talk about.

it's like a great colorful
and surprising painting
not hanging anywhere
else.

the stranger

he came in with
a knife in his
back, a pocket knife
sticking out
like a small branch,
and he had on a
small derby hat,
this sweaty round
face,
not a New Orleans face but
rather old European,
and Gus was playing
the guitar,
it was a yellow
varnished guitar,
and the man walked in
from the street
and fell across
a table
and somebody said,
"you son-of-a-bitch,"
and then somebody else
saw the knife
and said
"shit."

Gus put the
guitar
down.
the night was
really
ruined.

the other room

there is always somebody in the other room
listening beyond the wall.

there is always somebody in the other room
who wonders what you are doing
there without them.

there is always somebody in the other room
who is afraid you feel better being alone.

there is always somebody in the other room
who thinks you are thinking of someone else
or who thinks you don't care for anybody
except yourself in that other room.

there is always somebody in the other room
who no longer cares for you as much as they used
to.

there is always somebody in the other room
who is angry when you drop something
or who is displeased when you cough.

there is always somebody in the other room pretending
to read a book.

there is always somebody in the other room
talking for hours on the telephone.

there is always somebody in the other room
and you don't quite remember who it is
and you are surprised when they make a sound
or go down the hall to the bathroom.

but there isn't always somebody in the other
room because
sometimes there isn't another room.
and if there isn't
sometimes there isn't anybody here at
all.

the death of an era

my room was a block away.
I opened the bar at 5 a.m. and
closed it at
2 a.m.

often the dark and the light got
mixed up.
I'd be sitting there and it
would be last call.
then in a moment the sun
would be up and I'd still be
sitting there.

"Jim," I'd say to the bartender,
"I thought it was last
call."

at other times I'd find myself
in the bar full of people.
everybody would be
drinking and talking and I'd have a
drink in my hand.
I hardly knew any of the
people but it seemed like a
good time.
"hey, hey," I'd say.

5 years of that bar.
and nobody came and got
me.
but I wasn't crazy.
I just didn't know what
else to do.

one night I was sitting at
the bar
and somebody said,
"I smell smoke.
there's a fire somewhere."

"oh, it's here," I said.

a large flame was creeping up
my leg, a beautiful, curling
crackling red flame.

I reached down and patted
it out with my hand
which got burned all to
hell.

anybody else would have
sought medical
treatment.

we all just laughed and I got
a free drink.

actually, what got me out of
that bar
was the advent of
television
which was just coming
in.

after they put in the TV,
people were no longer the
entertainers.
they just sat together and
looked at the
screen.

I started drinking in my
room.
I drank and I drank and
I drank in my room.

one day I walked out
of that room,
got on a bus
and left the
city.

something had died
in America,
forever.

I had finished my 5 years
on that end
stool
just in
time.

for some friends

the sound of cunning
the sound of the sky and the sea.

the aperitif of a bitter night.
bitter friends who
argue who will speak the eulogy at the burial,
bitter half-men trying to steal your women,
bitter half-women letting themselves be stolen.

it took me 15 years to humanize poetry
but it's going to take more than me
to humanize humanity.

the good souls ain't gonna do it
anarchy ain't gonna do it
blacks
yellows
indians
chicanos
they ain't gonna do it.

I believe in the strength of the bloody hand
I believe in eternal ice
I demand that we die
blue-lipped and grinning across the impossibility
of ourselves
stretched across ourselves.

we meet, one time,
in a dark Barcelona cellar. but then
we drift apart. after
all, some people will fuck a lamppost in
the moonlight.

my eulogy? who will read it? will I even have a
grave? who will be happy at my
burial? one more god-damned genius
gone. idiots love to bury
gods.

meanwhile they hope that my typewriter fails,
that my love is less, that my hope is less,
that my pain is more.
ah, my friends all wish me the
best of things.

door-knocking ranting idiots
come ye all
to spew your special poison on me and upon
what little things are
mine.

little rat-children of the universe
enjoy the fact that I allowed you to insult me
enjoy the fact that I opened the door
enjoy the fact that I either grew old
or that I disappeared with time.

ah, my friends
my friends
my friends.

broken

there isn't any
justification
there isn't any
lie
any truth
any love ... there aren't any
tugboats, cats, dogs,
fish,
skies.

even your suffering is
a mirage.

there aren't any contracts
there isn't any honor
any principal,
and reason has gone
fishing in the
desert.

there isn't any rational basis
there isn't any nobility.

a broken shoelace
is the tragedy:
not the hands of me
strangling that
tiny place
you call
love.

wall clock

many years ago
in this one place where I worked
the man was big and black
very big and very black
his name was Whiplash.
nobody bothered him
neither the supervisors
the owners
nor the Mayor
of Washington, D.C.

it was late one night and I was
working next to him
when he asked me,
"hey, man, what time you got?"

I didn't look at him.
I took my finger and pointed
to the back wall
where there was a large clock.

"I wanna know *your* time, man, I
see you got a wristwatch there!"

I waited some moments. then
once again I pointed my finger at the
clock
and went back to work.

from then on
I was in tight
with Whiplash
and all the others.

they thought I had guts
that I knew no fear
but they had it all wrong.
it was just that I was frightened of
many more important things.

the beer bottle blow

it was a slow night in
Henry's Haven
when she walked in.
she was about 33 and
built like 33
brick shit houses.
there hadn't been a
woman like that in Henry's for
13 years.

when she sat down and
ordered a double whiskey
Henry said, "no charge,
baby."

she picked it
up and slugged it
down.

her hair was down all around
her face
stringy hair
unwashed
but she had other
great
attributes.

all the boys were
watching as Henry
refilled her glass.

"shit," she said,
"shit."

she didn't say
anything else.
she downed the
second drink
stood on her seat

with her
high heels
and stepped onto the
bar top.

she stood there
looking at the
boys.

"juke box,"
she said.

it was hard to
understand her
when she spoke
for as everybody could now
see
she had no teeth in
her mouth
but she was still only
33
and with all those other
great attributes
we didn't care.
somebody put a
coin in the juke box
and
she began a
very sexy dance
wiggling all over
lifting her
skirt.

"shake it, baby,
shake it!" one old
guy said.

"I'm harder than the
Rock of Gibraltar!"
said another old guy.

she began to
strip then.
off came the
dress.
then the
bra.

the juke box
stopped.

she stood there
and said,
"shit."

one of the old boys
leaped up
and inserted
another coin.

the panties came
off
and she
started doing
back bends,
spreading her
legs.

many of the boys
hadn't seen a
naked woman for
decades.

she could really
dance.
she stuck her
head
down
between her legs
reached up with her
hands and
spread the cheeks of
her ass.

then she
grabbed a beer bottle
got down on her
knees
and sucked it
off.

then
she climbed down off
the bar
found her
underthings
her clothing

got dressed
sat down on the
bar stool
again.

Henry kept refilling
her glass.
she kept drinking the
refills.

finally it was
2 a.m.

"Baby," Henry said,
"I gotta close up
but you can stay."

"stay?" she said.
"I'm gonna strip on the
sidewalk!"

she walked out and
everybody walked out
behind her
including Henry.

out there
on the street

she began stripping
all over again
she got her dress
off
she got her bra
off

and then
she reached down
and grabbed her
purse.
she pulled a gun
out of her
purse
pointed it
at the
sidewalk and
pulled the
trigger.

it went off

the bullet
ricocheted
and
got Henry
squarely in the
groin.

she put the gun
back into her
purse
and walked away down
the street
just in her
panties.

the cops didn't find
her
that night
or the next or
the next.

where can a woman
go
built like 33 brick shit
houses
dressed just in her
panties?

and you know what
they say about
no teeth in the
mouth.

some of my fathers

there was
the one in the Philly parts warehouse
who told us that
"today we will do the difficult and
tomorrow we will do the impossible!"
he was strong as an ox,
bright-eyed, walked
briskly and wore a well-pressed suit
every day.

and the one in the New York warehouse
who told me that when he started working
there his wife had to
wash and iron the same shirt
each night so that he could
wear it fresh the next day and
now he was foreman of the
paperback receiving
department.

and the one who managed the stock clerks at
Milliron's in L.A. and
who answered each and every demand,
"all right, o.k."
he was always poring over the inventory sheets
counting the uncountable
articles of clothing.
with his shining bald head he was
steady
not ambitious
quiet.
eyes like a hawk he had
quit trying long ago and
always answered the phone,
"all right, o.k." as he
sent stock boys running off to the various
floors
with orders to fill.
he was glued to those inventory forms,

bent over,
always counting.
"hey, Barth!" a voice would call, "they need 3
number nines down on
6!"
"all right, o.k."

and there was
the Mexican foreman in the railroad yard
watching me work sick through the days
after the long nights of cigarettes and drink
watching me silently
for days
his eyes on me alone
he never seemed to move
standing there on the same patch
of dried mud
until one day
he was right behind me
and I heard his voice
and I knew it was my Mexican
foreman
and he said,
"hey, Chinaski, you
fuck around too much!"

and the fat one,
Dan, not only fat but
big, big and fat, totally
brutal, an obscene stinking
hulk, bully brute bastard,
pushing his way up
from clerk
simply taking over
without promotion
without authority
quite amazing
ordering us all about
he just stopped clerking and began
supervising.
it was a gradual

day-by-day transformation
until it was too late
for all of us.
I never quite understood
how it had happened
nor was I interested.
I left for another
city
out of some life-saving
itch
then came back to that same
city
re-applied for my job
there
got it
went in the next morning
and there was Dan
back at his former station
as stock clerk
counting out little parts for
shipping.
he was very
subdued.
I said hello to the
other workers who
were still there
then said hello to
Dan.
he appeared to remember
me.
was fatter than ever
but somehow very different.
then a slim young
black boy in a green sweater
said,
"all right, let's all get back to
work."
"just saying 'hello' to some old friends,"
I told him.
"fine," he said, "now
you're done. get to
work."

and Zuckerman who came
jumping over the crates at
the rear of the loading dock
eyes
juiced, almost hysterical, trying to
catch a worker
slacking off.
"hey, what is it?" I asked
him, "you got the runs
or something?"
"that does it," he said,
"you're finished."
"no," I said, "you're
finished."
I put in a call to our
union rep. Randy Wood (who
wasn't worth a crap).
the 3 of us stood there.
"Randy," I told the
union man, "this fellow is
obviously unbalanced, he
jumps about and he screams
and the people here
are afraid to leave their
posts to
piss or to drink water."
"now Hank," said
Randy, "we are all
gentlemen and I'm sure there's
just a misunderstanding.
let's all shake
hands."
"I won't shake that hand,"
I said, "it's dirty,"
then went back and started
working again.
"what is it with that asshole
Zuckerman?" I asked my buddy
Big Daddy Hill at the
coffee break.
Big Daddy looked at me over

his styrofoam cup with his big brown eyes,
Big Daddy just looked at me and
didn't answer. and early
one morning after checking out
at 3:48 a.m.
I walked down the back alley
to the parking lot
and I noticed
patches of blood
fresh blood
bright and strange in the
moonlight and then I saw
a bloody handkerchief
and Zuckerman's jacket
and further up
the ambulance and
they were closing the doors with
Zuckerman
inside.
then
before I could get there
the ambulance moved
off
and there was nobody
around
when usually
at that time
there were 50 or 60
people coming off the
shift.

Stallings was easy.
Stallings was always trying to
fuck the secretaries.
he really pressured them
and he had no time to
fuck us.
so we did our jobs without
leadership.
we did our work early and fast
and had time to build little

shelters in the back of the
warehouse.
we had radios
fish tanks
pills
liquor
long breaks
but the pay wasn't good
so the boys started moving
stock out the rear door
stashing it in the alley in
garbage cans
and picking it up
late at night.
Stallings kept playing with the
secretaries
and then the boys found out that
Stallings was moving stuff
out the back too
only his garbage cans were
several yards up the
street.
inventory at that place
was a
joke:
there just wasn't much
to count.
but the business kept going
and the owner didn't
know or care what was
going on.
he still drove his
big new car
and had an impressive home
in the hills
and Stallings kept hiring new
young secretaries.

I guess the worst was
old Karl.
Karl was white but had

turned a strange light brown
toasted by the job
you might say.
he had been there
many years
and was respected and
thought to be
efficient,
his eyes faded to a dull unblinking
blue.
Karl became almost my second
father
and he told me,
"you know, there's not much
to it. you gotta find an easy
spot and lay down there. for
guys like you and me, you know, we've
got to accept. and after a while
you grow a shell and
then you grow a second shell and then
you grow a third shell and then it
gets comfortable."
Karl was a three-shelled turtle
he even looked like a
turtle—he had a turtle's head,
mouth, eyes.
but he was the worst, he was worse
than the brutes, worse than the
bosses, worse than the
workers
because he was dead inside.
but I'll say one thing
for him:
he knew what he was
and that's going a long way
in a hurry.
all he had left to do was
die
but I moved on first
and left him
there

respectfully crawling in
the dust.
but of all my bosses
he was as close somehow
as anyone
to that first father
who had fucked
my mother's pussy
so long ago
and who had created
all these troubles
for me.

black sun

Caresse Crosby published my first short story
when I was 24 and then other things like a
natural madness and depression got a
hold of me, and one night from somewhere in Georgia I wrote
a series of letters for help—not spiritual help
but asking for dollars for food and such until I could
figure out how to continue living as painlessly as possible.
having indifferent parents and no friends I mailed my
letters to literary strangers.
well, no money arrived. in fact, there were no replies, except
one
which followed me somehow through a series of cities
and towns
it reached me in New Orleans
and it was from Caresse and there was no money inside
but
the letter was nice: she said she was living in a
castle in Italy and helping the poor.
I had always been in love with the photos of two people:
Kay Boyle and Caresse Crosby.

if I had been Harry I would never have killed myself
as foolishly as he did
I would have stayed in bed with Caresse, drinking wine
and throwing darts at bullfight posters on the wall.

I never wrote to Kay Boyle because I ran out of stamps
but I'm sure she would have answered me too
if she'd had the chance.

the players

it's down at a track near the border and it's called
The Payoff Hotel. it's directly north of the track
perched on a cliff and after the races you can look
down at the deserted track and see the stables and now and
then a horse walking and always those stacks of hay.

there are hundreds of rooms, all full, each room with
a shower and black-and-white tv.
next to the lobby is a dance floor where some of the older
players dance and romance the few young girls
to the loud music of a small band playing yesterday's forgotten
melodies.

the players drink beer and cheap wine, their shirttails
hang out, their pants are too short, their shoes badly worn
down at the heels.

walking through the halls at night, most of the doors stand
open and in each room sits one or two men reading the day's
        race results
and drinking beer and wine, and in the morning by the pool
before the races some of them will be dressed in sporty
trunks but they'll each have their carefully
folded copy of *The Daily Racing Form.*

there aren't any steady winners at The Payoff Hotel.
how they exist from season to season is unknown but
the players are strangely durable
and all the rooms are always taken.

I'll see you there next summer and I won't be able to tell
you from them and I'll look like
you and none of us will look very good as we all stand and
hope for that real, live action.

batting slump

the sun slides down through the shades.
I have a pair of black shoes and a pair of
brown shoes.
I can hardly remember the girls of my youth.
there is numb blood pulsing through the
falcon and the hyena and the pimp
and there's no escaping this unreasonable
sorrow.
there's crabgrass and razor wire and the snoring
of my cat.
there are lifeguards sitting in canvas-back chairs
with salt rotting under their toenails.
there's the hunter with eyes like rose
petals.
sorrow, yes, it pulls at me
I don't know why.
avenues of despair slide into my ears.
the worms won't sing.
the Babe swings again
missing a 3-and-2 pitch
twisting around himself
leaning over his
whiskey gut.
cows give milk
dentists pull teeth
thermometers work.

I can sing the blues
it doesn't cost a dime and
when I lay down tonight
pull up the covers
there's the dark factor
there's the unknown factor
there's this manufactured
staggering
black
empty
space.

I got to hit one out of here
pretty soon.

somewhere it's 12:41 a.m.

the soprano sings in my radio
on this red red night
and the sky is scraped
raw.
I bite on a toothpick and pretend
immortality.
it's all so fair and so awful, it's all so
awfully fair.
to think, I've never been to London.
I sit here in fat soft slippers and
muse upon that.
but not for long in this
red red night.
you know, I might easily let the
monsters have my
brain,
but once you let them in, getting
them out is almost
impossible.
now the soprano is gone.
now it's a baritone.
he sings to me of this dark dark
night.
he seems to be locked in
dark red walls.
I shift in my chair, spit out the
toothpick.
dark dark night.
red red night.
my feet walk in cosmic
dust
and foolishness
survives.

the reply

green dogs, dinosaur sky, serpent of hope,
these walls like blades;
the streets like shriveled teats on
dead monkeys;
the false friends, these hands, the dead books,
this lock, this stinking lock;

the blue donkey with grapes for eyes
this pint of grape juice like bile
the jeweled dagger sticking out of
my back
how did I end up like this?
slump-shouldered in brownwhite doom.

it's your own fault, they will say,
their precious elephantine mouths
packed with blood and
dust.

searching for what?

as one goes to the racetrack year after year one notices
certain individuals who are there every day,
people who are strangely dressed and as desperate of eye
as I am.
there was one who stank badly and had diseased
skin.
I often picked him up as he hitchhiked in and I believe
he slept in the bushes along the freeway.
his theory was that all the jockeys got together
before the races and decided which number would
win that day—they chose a number and only that number
        would
win all day long and that's why all those sons-of-bitches
were rich: they all simply bet that number.

and there was another guy I had seen for years at all the
tracks, I was in a hurry and he bumped me with his elbow
and I said, "hey, Mac, watch that shit!" and he said,
"I got a mind to rub your face in the cement!" and I said,
"wait a minute," and I took my coat off and laid it on
a bench but when I turned around he was gone.
I still see him at the track and the strangest thing is
that he seems to be getting thinner and weaker as by
        comparison
I seem to get younger and stronger, but I don't think
it's my imagination, I think he must be having
a long string of losers.

then there's the blonde, she was fat and slow but it
didn't seem to matter, she had a way of picking winners,
and some of the winners were longshots, day after day, she
bet the horses calmly in a very offhand manner and now
I see her in the clubhouse, dressed fine, still fat,
with some young guy at her side,
and she knows that I know but I don't say anything. since
I'm in the clubhouse too maybe I've done some whoring
in my own way.

there's another one, dresses dapper, smokes good cigars,

but he never bets, he just pokes around in the
trashcans, reaching his fingers down into all the
wet coffee containers, napkins, ripped tickets, old news-
papers, stale hot dog buns, beer puke, he just reaches down in
there, inhaling on his cigar, searching for what?

then there's one who starts running when he sees a late flash
on the board, they are putting them into the gate and
he starts running to the window like he's had a message
from heaven, and he's right, the last flash of the board
is the most important but you can't win that way either,
he's poorly dressed and desperate and come to think of it I
haven't seen him for some weeks now.

I think I've been around the track longer than any of
the other bettors, maybe not longer than the hot walkers,
the trainers or the jocks, they've been there longer
than me, but not the bettors.

all my women (and there have been plenty of them) have said
(with one voice) "my God, every time I see you
you start talking about the HORSES! you'll talk about the
     HORSES
for hours! my God, what a dull man you are! and then you
     write
POEMS about the HORSES! don't you realize how dull
your HORSE poems are? nobody understands them!"

here's another.

the hero and the shortstop

the Babe would get drunk and
dangle Rabbit
out the 12th floor hotel window
by his ankles
and Rabbit would say,
"you son-of-a-bitch!
when I get back into the room
I'll kill you!"
the Babe would laugh
at his little roommate
he was the hero
he could hit a homer
any time
he really wanted to.
the Rabbit played short,
was always hitting around
.222
but the hits he took away
from the other teams
really made him
in a sense
a .500 batter.

and the next day
they'd be down on the ball field
together
hung over
and doing it
as well as anyone has
ever done it
all over again.

there are some people who just
do things very well
without even thinking
about it, and then you have
all the others.

my favorite movie

I used to like the guy who played the piano
with his drink on the lid in some honky-tonk
bar in China or Manila or some tropical island
    somewhere.
cigarette dangling while the dope dealers,
killers and international spies go about
scratching their calves in the smoky
heat as they decide the fate of whores and
nations
the piano player tickles out a tune
while a honey-eyed blonde in a banana-colored
dress
v-neck to bellybutton
eyebrows plucked away
leans against the piano like a limp decibel
elbows like clothespins.
she sings as
the stranger comes in
the tough handsome one
the short-spoken one
with sweated collarband
after some heroic battle with evil dumb
nazis.
the stranger
nods through squinted eyes
at the piano player
who nods back as
the stranger and the singer walk off to
a back room
together.

the piano player then moves slowly into another
tune and I used to think, jesus, he should have
her, but he's certainly not in a hurry
about anything, seems to have more sense than most, he
doesn't worry about nazis or a better world
or how to act tough enough to deserve a woman
in a banana dress;
he has that satisfied smile,

wears old-fashioned and comfort-
able suspenders and you realize all he finally wants
is that drink on the piano and
then to play another tune, he knows the price of every-
thing else:
too much.

the piano player seems content enough
and then somebody asks for
a new tune and he runs it off, first sipping the
drink, lighting a cigarette, and then his fingers
run up and down the keys, up and down, it's
good and easy, it asks for nothing, asks for so little
that it gives hope to all those who also ask
for no chance, who ask for nothing at all,
who just ask for someplace to sit quietly and wait
for the slanting sun moving on the wall
and for the peace of soft rain
spread out all over the place.

share the pain

got pissed with my landlord and landlady
because there was nothing else to
do.

you shouldn't have all those whores and freaks
hanging around your place,
my landlady said.

the landlord and I
stepped out to fight. he got me around the neck
and I banged his belly and
we ran into a tree
and then she stopped the fight
when we broke the tree down.

I could kill you, said my landlord,
but what's the
use? you're my tenant.

thanks sport, I
said.

we went back inside and sat down
and the landlord had a big bowl in
the center of the table.
he poured in some whiskey and he poured in
some wine and he poured in some ale
and then he poured in 2 quarts of
7-Up.

he might as well have thrown in the
alka-seltzers
too.

the tits hang low on the cow, I said,
and my land is your
land.

you damn fool, said my landlady, whatta you

know about cows? I don't think you ever been
on a farm.

yes, ma'am, I said, no, I mean,
no ma'am.

go ahead, said my landlord, dip in and get a cupful
to drink.

like a damn fool, I did. the revolution was a slow-
time coming.

the old pinch hitter

comes out of the dugout in the last of the 9th.
2 out. the winning run on 2nd base.
he's 7-for-20 in this young season: .350
he walks slowly to the plate, seems relaxed but
deliberate. faces a fireballing young pitcher
18 years younger than he is.
takes ball one. ball two. fouls off
the next two. then runs it to 3-and-2.
the fireballer gets his sign, checks 2nd
blazes it in as the runner goes
the perfect pitch
the perfect strike
knee-high and inside:
click!
nobody can handle it:
a solid liner between 1st and 2nd
the runner from 2nd scores.
the old pinch hitter touches first
then turns and walks slowly toward
the dugout.
another night's work.
that shower is going to feel
good.

ah, ah, ah

I suppose that what disturbs me about the sages,
the great minds,
is that they are so sure of what they
say.
yet I have to forgive them.
I admire their energy.
(I too have energy but it's not for
finding answers.)

instead of knowing more and more
I know less and less.

instead of becoming more comfortable
I become more
anguished.

jesus, I am beginning to sound like
one of those philosophy books in the library
that runs around in circles
like a dog chasing its
tail.

I suppose that what I liked about the libraries
back then when I was young
were the old bums
shitting in the crappers and washing their hands and
faces
and then falling asleep over a book
their noses inside the books
and they were asleep
and the flies circled them
as the bindings of 100,000 dull books
stared at me.

all the sages
all the years
wasted.

Edith sent us

you just get home from the track
after losing
and taking the wrong freeway (again)
lost in the dark
the workers roaring home around you
eager to get to their tv sets.
you feel subnormal,
idiotic,
real people don't get lost on
freeways.
you finally get off the wrong one and
onto the right one (#7)
onto #405
onto the Harbor Freeway
then onto the Hollywood Freeway,
off at Silverlake for your 3 bottles of
wine.
then down Hollywood Blvd.
to your street where you turn and park.
a book of poems in the mail.
you read 5 or 6 poems in the bathtub
then hurl the book from the tub into the wastebasket
get out, towel, then into the yellow robe eager
for the first drink.
there is a banging on the door.
they want to see you.
2 boys with motorcycle helmets.
"Edith sent us," says the tall one,
"she said she knew you and it was o.k. for us
to drop by anytime we were in town."
"I don't know any Edith," you tell them.
"we thought we'd get a case of beer and talk,"
he says.
"look," you say, "I just got knifed
at the track. I even got lost on the freeway.
I was just going to have my first drink. I'm
tired. I was going to relax..."
you gesture toward the glass of wine waiting by the
typer.

"we thought we'd get a case of beer and
talk," he says.
the short one never says anything, he just
looks.
"I'm *tired,* don't you see?"
"well," he says, "suppose we come by next Saturday
with a case of beer when you're not
so beat?"
"no," you say, "I just can't
do it."
they leave, into the night with their helmets.
they'll get on those freeways
they'll roar in and out
angling through racing steel without
doubt or fear or confusion.
they don't need you.

finally
you sit down.
the first drink, as always, is
the best.

we're all gonna make it

my black buddy Rice
I got him hooked
on the horses.
we worked nights
at the post office
and I'd see him
at the track
during the day
and we'd come in
each night
burned out and
broke
the dream right
down the crapper.

and
speaking of
the crapper
several times
I saw him there
in the crapper
with his buddies
and he was doing
a little dance
in there
singing, "scooby
doobie do ..."
as if
everything was really
all right.

but it wasn't
all right
and he didn't
want the boys
to know that
it wasn't.

I felt bad

for him
putting on his
act
there
for his brothers
before the
crapper mirror
as if
he
was making it
big at the
track.

well,
you know,
there was nothing much
happening there in East L.A.
anyhow.
most of the fellows
(black and white)
had wives
they were tired
of
and the wives they
were
tired of them too
and tired of the
unpaid bills and the
children.

Rice soon became
the inspiration
for his black brothers
their hope to also score
their walnut
their ace of spades.

anyhow, one night
after his crapper
dance
a few hours

later
in his car
on our
30-minute
lunch:
(2 tall cans of
beer
apiece)
I told him:
"hey, look, Rice,
you don't have to
perform for
them, just
be cool or
do it just
for yourself..."
"look, Hank,"
he told me,
"I'm gonna stay
black until I
make it."

"what do you
mean?" I asked
him.

"I mean,
I'm going
to be
black until I'm
drinking
with you and
all those beautiful
white whores up there
at the
Beverly Hills
Hotel..."

as it turned
out
(sadly)

the beautiful white call girls
up there at the Beverly
Hills Hotel
never
got the chance
to drink with
either one of
us.

"scooby doobie
do ..."

hymn from the hurricane

paid my dues in Macon, went crazy in Tennessee,
found the love of God in St. Louis,
got the hell out of *there*.
found the whore with the heart of gold in Glendale,
ran away from that.
floundered awhile along the Mason-Dixon Line,
came to my senses in New Orleans.
mailed a letter home, and got knocked on my ass in Houston.
started sitting at the center of the bar instead of at the end.
got rolled 3 times in a row somewhere near the Appalachians.
married a woman with a crippled neck who died unclaimed in India.
name of the first horse I ever bet on was Royal Serenade who died
long ago.
what glistens best for me is the first drink of the night.
I will hear forever the wheels of the Greyhound bus carrying me
        to nowhere.
J. Cash sang "*I killed a man in Reno just to watch him die*" as the
cons cheered.
celled with public enemy no. one in Moyamensing Prison (he
snored at night).
my women tell me that I am insane because of my parents.
sometimes I feel like a motherless child.
my favorite color is yellow and my backbone is the same.
nine-tenths of Humanity embraces self-pity and the other tenth
makes them look pitiful.
the rat and the roach are the most powerful reminders of
        enduring life.
what was always best for me was seeing fear in the eyes of the
        bully.
the saddest thing was old women watering geraniums at 2 p.m.
and what I learned was to do it *now* in spite of the consequences.
and what I also learned was that something once said could
quickly become untrue.

I paid my dues in Macon and went crazy in Tennessee,
found myself on the 2nd floor of a hotel in Albuquerque (the bed
bugs ate well).
found myself on a track gang going west and didn't yearn for
a seat in Congress.
I remember the girl who showed me her panties when I was 8
        years old.

I remember the red streetcars, and the vacant lots between
the houses in Los Angeles.
I remember that the girl who showed her panties to half the town
    had
showed me first.
I was always a coward who didn't care.
I was always a brave man who didn't try to win.
I found that screwing women was a social duty like making
    money.

I paid my dues in Tennessee and went crazy in Macon.

I had no idea of the black-white game and
sat in the back of a streetcar in New Orleans.
I hate politics and I hate the obvious answers.
I paid my dues in East Kansas City.
I beat hell out of a 6-foot-4 240-pound guy in Philly.
I stayed on the floor in Miami after a 150-pounder decked me
with his first punch.
the state of the mind is the State of the Union.
what you want to do and what you've got to do is the same thing.
I once watched a sailor fight an alligator and the alligator quit.

only boring people are bored.
only the wrong flags fly.
the person who tells you they are not God really thinks otherwise.
God is the invention of failures.
the only hell is where you are.

passed through Dallas and rammed through Pasadena.
I never paid my dues because there was nobody to collect them.
I've smashed two full-length mirrors and they are still looking for
    me.
I've walked into places where no man should ever go.
I've been mercilessly beaten and left for dead.
I have lumps all over my skull from blackjacks and etc.
the angels pissed themselves in fear.
I am a beautiful person.

and you are.
and she is.
as is the yellow thumping of the sun and the glory of the world.

2

flight time to nowhere

soundless

it is said
that in the courting stage
the man
does most of the talking.

when the male and female
begin living together
or
get married
the female
begins to talk more and more
and as the affair continues
the male
talks less and less
and
it is believed
that in many cases
the male
lapses entirely into
silence
he is
like some dumb beast
with its tongue plucked out
forever.

miracle man

in this neighborhood
about 4 blocks north
and 2 south
sits a small house
paint peeling
and
weeds growing
in the front
yard

and
all around this
house
are
other houses
with
perfect
green lawns
trimmed hedges
flowers
and
polished autos
sitting
in the drives.

"I like this
guy," I tell my woman.
"I'd sure like to
see him, you know, see
what he looks
like."

"I've seen him,"
says my woman.

"yeah? yeah? how?
when?"

"twice. and each time

it was the same. he
was just sitting in
his window and he
had his hat on and
pulled down low
over his eyes."

"beautiful," I say,
"beautiful."

I keep
driving by
hoping
to see him
for myself
but
I never do.
anyhow,
for me
he's the salvation
of this neighborhood.

it's when people
are
all the same
that
everything gets named and useless

and here's
this saint
without a name.

little theater in Hollywood

they didn't have change for $20 so
we ran to the nearest
bar
had drinks
ran back. they
had started. they
were all too young, Sade was too
young, Marat was too
young, the mad people were too
young, the girl who knifed Marat in the bath was too
young, but the audience was
old, overfed and not particularly
bothered—lost off the highway
of life
the whole pack of them just
looking for something to
do.

the audience talked throughout the
play, laughing in all the wrong
places.
that audience and those actors
deserved each
other.

at intermission
there was a small coffee urn
in the lobby
(2 bits a cup)
the audience pressed forward
too ungentle to form a
line, too busy eyeing each other
thinking,
maybe somebody is here
who will recognize
me.

we ran again to the bar.
2 quick ones and

when we got back they had begun
again. and the kindest thing I can say
about it
all
is that nobody tried to steal the show
not even the
actors.

and leaving, getting
outside, finding the
car
you felt like you had gotten away from
something unreal,
and later in bed
there wasn't much to say.
we laughed
then. $5.00 a
head, it was worth that, perhaps something
learned after
all. (I'd been to boxing matches and bullfights
and come away feeling
worse.)

simple failure can be found
everywhere, in
the hospitals and in
the schools and in
the asylums and at the jails
and in the dust
of the road.

we slept
then.
the drinks had been the best part
of it all.

novels

the older sister of the woman I was going with
was fat.
she was fat with flesh and fat with novels.
she wrote a novel every six months
which she would mail to a New York editor
who advertised his services in writers'
magazines.
he'd charge her $300,
send her 3 pages of useless criticism
and she'd start a new novel.

she fell in love with every man she went
to bed with.
she was always in love.

her younger sister made me read her novels.
her younger sister had a nice ass
so I read the novels.
but the older sister who wrote,
her life was far more interesting than
her novels—for example
take the last man who came along.
he was a charmer,
he had no job
but he would
sing when he got drunk
and we all thought that he had a beautiful
voice.
so the fat sister paid to send him
part-time to a
broadcasting school.

he drank beer at night
went to school in the morning
bullied her 3 children in the afternoon
while I drank beer night and day
and fucked the other sister.

the fat sister then had the last of his

teeth pulled and got him a set of
beautiful false teeth to help him with his
broadcasting.

later he got a job, not broadcasting,
but driving a beer truck
and the fat sister got pregnant
and he sat around drinking beer
during her pregnancy
because he'd lost the job on the
beer truck.
he finally found a job as a fry cook
at the local eatery but
then the baby came and he vanished
when he saw the hospital bill.

but she never wrote a novel about it
all.
"why don't you write a novel about all
that?" I asked her.
"Hank," she answered, "you're just a
cynical old drunk and a son-of-a-bitch.
no wonder your stuff sounds like it was
written in a cesspool."

the next novel she wrote had a cynical
old drunk in it who thought he could write but he
couldn't really write at all, he just wrote shit
which appealed somehow to the mundane appetite
of the masses.

it was not long after that
that the other sister and I split
and that was the end of the whole sad
story.

pleased to meet you

"oh my god," she says, "Jean Don Carlo!
he doesn't speak English
he says *everything*
with his eyes!"

"ah, bullshit," you say.

"no," she says, "he's devastatingly charming,
even *you* would like him!"

it was only a slight conversation
only a bit of slight conversation
and then a year elapses ...

one night you walk into a small party
with her
and there are various introductions
and then she says,
"and this is Jean Don Carlo!"

hello.
hello.

pleased.
pleased.

you shake hands.

Jean Don Carlo
has almost no chin
his eyes are big and round and empty
no charm there
nothing.

even when he stands or sits down
it is like nothing standing there or
sitting down.

and the night offers nothing dramatic

to transform him
although he now speaks
some English.

he makes his living selling French
racing bikes in America.

the other people also stand or sit around and there
is nothing to do but drink...

on the drive back in
you say nothing to her about Jean Don Carlo
and she says nothing to you
about Jean Don Carlo
and that's very good
except that you wonder about all the things
she had told you
and then you let that go too
because nothing is really that meaningful
or important
anymore.

next time she'll have something else to say
about a new rock group or a new vitamin
or a way to achieve suspended animation forever
in a polished steel cylinder
for only $35 a day where
you are not touched by
atmospheric decay.

It's ALWAYS been the Jean Don Carlos
of the world
with their pants down and
nothing to show for it.

yes, I am

no matter what woman I'm with
people ask me,
are you still with her?

my average relationship lasts
two-and-one-half years:
with war
inflation
unemployment
alcoholism
gambling
minor poverty
and my own degenerate personality
I think I do well enough.

I like reading the Sunday papers in bed with her.
I like orange ribbons tied around the cat's neck.
I like sleeping up against a body that I know well.
I like black slips tossed on the foot of my bed
at 2 in the afternoon.
I like seeing how the photos turned out.

I like to be helped through the holidays:
4th of July, Labor Day, Halloween, Thanksgiving,
Christmas, New Year's.
women know best how to ride those rapids
and they are less afraid of love than I am.

my women make me laugh where professional comedians
fail.

there is the comfort of walking out to buy a
newspaper together.

I take much pleasure in being alone
but there is also a strange warm grace in not being alone.

I like sharing boiled red potatoes late at night.

I like eyes and fingers keener than mine that can
untie the knots in my shoelaces.

I like letting her drive the car on dark nights
when the road and the way are too much for me.
the car radio on
we light cigarettes and talk about small things
and now and then we
fall silent.

I like hairpins left on the table and
on the bathroom floor.
I like sharing these same walls with
the same woman.

I dislike the insane and useless fights which sometimes
occur
and I dislike myself at those times
giving nothing
understanding nothing.

alone or together
I like boiled asparagus
and radishes
and green onions.
I like running my car through a car wash.
I like it when I have $10 to win on a six-to-one
shot.
I like my little radio which plays
Shostakovich, Brahms, Beethoven, Mahler.

but I also like it when there's a knock on the door and
she's there.

no matter what woman I'm with
people ask me,
are you still with her?

they must think I bury them
one at a time in
the Hollywood Hills.

now she's free

Cleo's going to make it now
she's got her shit together
she split with Barney
Barney wasn't good for her
she got a bigger apartment
furnished it beautifully
and bought a new silver Camaro
she works afternoons in a dance joint
drives 30 miles to the job from
Redondo Beach
goes to night school
helps out at the AIDS clinic
reads the *I Ching*
does Yoga
is living with a 20-year-old boy
eats health food
Barney wasn't good for her
she's got her shit together now
she's into T.M.
but she's the same old fun-loving Cleo
she's painted her nails green
got a butterfly tattoo
I saw her yesterday
in her new silver Camaro
her long blonde hair blowing
in the wind.
poor Barney.
he just doesn't know what he's
missing.

we get along

the various women I have lived with have loved
rock concerts, reggae festivals, love-ins, peace
marches, movies, garage sales, fairs, political rallies,
weddings, funerals, poetry readings, Spanish classes,
spas, parties, bars and so forth.

while I have lived with this
machine.

while the ladies attended social functions, saved the
whales, the seals, the dolphins, the great white shark,
and while the ladies talked on the telephone

this machine and I lived here
together.

as we are living together here tonight: this machine, the 3
cats, the radio and little else.

after I die the ladies will say (if asked): "he just
liked to sleep and drink; he never wanted to go
anywhere. well, maybe to the racetrack, *that* stupid
place!"

the ladies I have known and lived with have been
very social, jumping into their cars, waving, rushing
off as if some experience of great import
awaited them:

"It's a new-wave punk group, they're great!"

"Allen Ginsberg's reading!"

"I'm late for my dance class!"

"I'm going to play Scrabble with Rita!"

"It's a surprise birthday party for Fran!"

meanwhile I have this machine.
this machine and I we really live
together.

Olympia, that's her name.

a good girl.

nearly almost always
faithful.

swinging from the hook

often while driving down the freeway I feel like
putting my head down on the steering wheel and closing my
eyes, or in the supermarket while the girl is
tabulating the sale suddenly I feel like reaching out and
tearing her dress away so that I can see her
breasts, and
often in the mornings when I awaken I don't feel
like getting up and dressing and
doing what must be done, instead I feel
like staying in bed for 3 or 4 days and nights
or
often when I have stopped at a red light
and there aren't any other cars around I have this
urge to plunge through the red light
and then when I get that thought I wonder why it is
that
I am allowed to drive my car at all?
it doesn't seem right that I am allowed to turn and
stop and start and speed just like
that old lady in the green Ford and blue hat I
saw a few hours ago as we passed each other on a
steep hill.
or sometimes at night I awaken and sit
and stare out the window at the
night but meanwhile I can feel my confusion sitting
there next to me, piled up like a stack of old
rubber tires.
and sometimes when I am copulating
I think, what am I doing copulating?
I am spooked continually by having to accomplish all the
ordinary things, the little things most people can do so
easily.
I sit here now at 12:09 a.m. and I want to
light this cigarette and I keep picking up the same
5 or 6 empty matchbooks, opening them and staring at
nothing at all. somebody else would own a cigarette
lighter, somebody else would be quietly sleeping, instead
I suddenly remember an insane woman I lived with
for 3 years who could do all the tiny things easily,
without even thinking, without confusion, and still probably
can.

AIDS

the easy days of sex are over,
sex is almost finished
here on earth
unless they are able to cure
what is killing
us.

the young will never know
how recklessly we went
from bed to bed,
from body to body,
from night to night.
it all, at times, became a
bore.

I wonder what we will lose
next?

it's been a hell of a
half century:
first the atom bomb,
then
this.

it's time for an invasion
of Space Aliens.

and they can damn well
have
it
all.

flight time to nowhere

we are sitting together in the airport bar
and I wave to the waitress for another two
drinks.

he says to me, the idea is to get
enough sun and enough rest and to always
pay the electric bill and the rent and/or
the mortgage on time.

two of the same, I tell the waitress.

and, he says, don't let the telephone company
overcharge you, watch for the police
in the rearview mirror and think about
exercising but don't do it.

how's your wife? I ask him. you know,
she's really a looker.

keep discarding your friends, he says, because
otherwise you are going to have to continue
loaning money to more and more people.

are you catching this flight with me?
I ask.

learn, he says, that there will be hours, days
and months ahead of feeling absolutely terrible
and that nothing can change that; neither new
girlfriends, health professionals,
changes of diet, dope, humility or
God.

the waitress has brought us our drinks, I
remind him.

wipe your ass good, he says, lifting his, and sleep
on your left side as much as possible.

I'll try, I tell him.

you will find, he says, that the most interesting
reading is not classics but the daily
newspaper.

pardon me, I tell him, but I've been paying for
all the drinks so far—

never apologize! he tells me. and never say
"thank you" or "good morning."
cultivate your prejudices, they are real.
never attempt to understand the other point of view
and treat your relatives like dogs. they
are. you owe them nothing.

you want another drink? I ask.

you must stay away, he says, from people who grow
their own grass, and stay away from writers, musicians,
singers and ballet dancers. painters are o.k. also
professional boxers and amateur plumbers.

waitress, I say, two more drinks.

and, he says, when somebody hates you, realize that
it's not personal, it's because you have something
that they don't have.

is there more? I ask.

there is much more, he says, such as
don't give advice, and if you are offered some
reverse it to find the
truth...

please shut up, I think to myself, this poem must
end now
here at the bottom of the page.

a woman in orange

I am frightened and
hung over crossing Rowena Avenue.

she drives wildly,
scratches herself under the
left arm.

"kids drive early where I come
from. my sister drove off a bridge when
she was 13 years old. our parents
never said anything."

she speeds through a red
light
the dog in the back seat
scratches himself.

now I'm frightened and hung over on
Hyperion Avenue.

then I'm frightened and hung over on
Sunset Boulevard.

the Vista Theatre says:
OPEN ALL NIGHT
GIRLS
        AS YOU LIKE TO
        SEE THEM
FOR UNSHOCKABLE ADULTS
        ONLY.

here's Rodney Drive.

there's an old woman in a
green hat.

there's all these other
cars.

there's a woman in orange
on the sidewalk
down on both knees.

what the hell
maybe I could join her?

better than
being
frightened and hung over
all over
again.

a poem for swingers

I like women who haven't lived with too many men.
I don't expect virginity but I simply prefer women
who haven't been rubbed raw by experience.

there is a quality about women who choose
men sparingly;
it appears in their walk
in their eyes
in their laughter and in their
gentle hearts.

women who have had too many men
seem to choose the next one
out of revenge rather than with
feeling.

when you play the field selfishly everything
works against you:
one can't insist on love or
demand affection.
you're finally left with whatever
you have been willing to give
which often is:
nothing.

some women are delicate things
some women are delicious and
wondrous.

if you want to piss on the sun
go ahead
but please leave the good women
alone.

backups

in this modern age of love/sex
relationships
we are all very clever.

in case we don't work, she tells me,
I have 4 backups.

4? well, that's good, I say.

how many you got? she asks.

well, now—

one and
two and, ah, there's, yes, 3,
and the one in Berkeley, that's 4,
and there's yes, there's
5. 5, that's
it.

I stare at her.

she blinks.

merry, merry

now let's see
who's on my Christmas list:
there are the 3 angry ladies
who've told me never
to call them again
and there's the guy down at
Jiffy-Lube who said he didn't have
time to give me an oil change
yesterday
and there's that black guy
at the toll bridge
who took it personal
when I was only jiving.
there's the guy who sold me
this house
who put in his own plumbing
and wiring.
there's the macho guy who got
8 million for fighting the champ
and quit because he said
he had stomach cramps.
and there's the jock
the other day
who wouldn't take
the opening on the rail
when I had him $20 win,
$20 place,
and then there are all the people
who will come by on Christmas Day
or the day before
or the day after
because it's the Season.
and then there are all the neighbors
who won't speak to me
because they heard me the other
night
as I ran through my front yard
drunk and naked and cursing,
throwing rocks.

then there are all the clerks
at checkout counters everywhere
who look like plastic statues
as I stand in their long lines
trying to hold back a
bowel movement.

and then, my friend, there's
you.

liberated woman and liberated man

look there.
the one you considered killing yourself
for.
you saw her the other day
getting out of her car
in the Safeway parking lot.
she was wearing a torn green
dress and old dirty
boots
her face raw with living.
she saw you
so you walked over
and spoke and then
listened.
her hair did not glisten
her eyes and her conversation were
dull.
where was she?
where had she gone?
the one you were going to kill yourself
for?

the conversation finished
she walked into the store
and you looked at her automobile
and even that
which used to drive up and park
in front of your door
with such verve and in a spirit of
adventure
now looked
like a junkyard
joke.

you decide not to shop at
Safeway
you'll drive 6 blocks
east and buy what you need
at Ralphs.

getting into your car
you are quite pleased that
you didn't
kill yourself;
everything is delightful and
the air is clear.
your hands on the wheel,
you grin as you check for traffic in
the rearview mirror.

my man, you think,
you've saved yourself
for somebody else, but
who?

a slim young creature walks by
in a miniskirt and sandals
showing a marvelous leg.
she's going in to shop at Safeway
too.

you turn off the engine and
follow her in.

a place to go

you can take your girlfriend who is wearing
a red hat
on any given day
whether you are feeling good or
not
you can sit out in the open
at this nice place
on the docks
and pick yourself out a spider crab
for $4.20 a pound
fresh and alive
(they will cook it for you)
watch those commercial fishboats
out there
take your crab and the sauce and a
wooden hammer and a sheet of
newspaper
to the thick wooden slivered table
crack your spider crab in the sun
and drink your beer.
the people around you are
normal and tired and easy.
the sun shines through the beer.
shit, it's been a hard day.
yeah, hammer that spider
everything is so perfect
you don't even have to argue with
your girlfriend.

age and youth

I was driving over a bridge when
I got this unfamiliar station
on the radio
and here was this older man
talking to a lady doctor.

"Doctor Stacey," he said,
"my wife is going through a
change of life.
she doesn't think she is
but she is."

this old guy had a soft
whiney voice.

"yes, go on," said Dr.
Stacey.

"well, Doctor, after 24 years of
marriage she is going out
with a younger man...
I'm older and he's young
and I think
she's trying to replace me
with him.
she says she loves me
but she keeps going out
with him."

I was on my way to Los
Alamitos racetrack.
I crossed over the bridge
and turned onto my favorite expressway.
a clear view for miles
to watch for police cars.
I opened it up to 75, then 80,
then 85.

"Doctor, this man drinks too much

and my wife says
if he keeps on drinking
she is going to leave
him
but he hasn't stopped drinking
she's still going out with
him.
I've lost weight, I've lost
several jobs, I can't
concentrate."

"I see," said Dr.
Stacey.

I had it up to
90.

"... my wife keeps
dating this man but she
still keeps dating me ..."

how romantic, I thought,
here's a man
who dates
his wife.

"... my last job
took me back east.
I sent her money
to come stay with me
for a week and
she seemed happy,
she said she loved
me but when we
came back
she began seeing
him again. then
I lost that job, I
couldn't concentrate ..."

I dropped the car back to

60 and lit a
cigarette.

"you evidently have a deep
need for your wife," Dr.
Stacey told the guy.

"I love her, Doctor, but she
is causing me
misery and anguish.
she's crucifying me
just like
my first wife did."

"oh," asked Dr. Stacey,
"were you married
before?"

the radio was fading in
and out, getting dimmer.
I wanted to hear what
the Doctor was going to tell
him.

I reached down to
fine-tune it
but
as I did so
I lost the station
entirely.

I drove along
trying to get it
back
working at the
knobs
but I kept getting
other stations—
music, news,
religious fanatics.
it was useless.

I turned the radio
off.

I had an idea
about what Dr. Stacey would
tell the old guy
as I hit Willow Street and
took a right: "if you
love her enough
just have patience
and faith, just wait
and endure
and when her fling is
over
she'll come back to you
she'll realize where
the real thing is."

that is crap, Dr. Stacey,
I said to myself,
he ought to
dump her butt
on the doorstep
of the young guy's place
go get drunk and
find a cathouse,
hire a housekeeper
with a big ass
and a Swedish
accent
and play cribbage
with her.

having resolved all
that
I drove on to the
racetrack
feeling mighty
pleased with
myself.

a good show

Rena had 30 pairs of high-heeled shoes on the floor
in the crapper and lived with Rickey in the front apartment.
with *New York* magazine on the coffee table we'd toke
with the eternal stereo in high gear.
Rena worked as a nudie dancer, hostess, so forth, while
Rickey dealt weed, and after an hour or so Rena would begin
her act, coming out first in a Frederick's outfit, dancing.
"Jesus, Jesus, look at that!" I'd holler and she'd
whirl about, vanish, then come back in another Frederick's
outfit, higher heels, more breast and ass showing.
"Jesus! oh my god!" I'd say, "I can't STAND it!" Rena would
slip into my lap and Rickey would flash the camera.
"oh, my god," I'd think, "I'm really LIVING!"

those nights were truly funny, sexy, mad, I'm not
sure they appreciated that; my girlfriend didn't: she broke
one of Rena's fingers when Rickey showed her the photos.

Rena and Rickey split and Rena used to come by and see
me with her new men, guys with earrings, chains, shirts
open to the waist, hairy, peripheral and dull.
then she started coming by alone: "guys are
assholes!" she'd say.

I could never make a move on Rena, she looked damn good
but I just didn't have the taste for her; she was
honest and funny and crazy, quite wonderful, but I
just couldn't make a move on her. I think she finally
realized that.
then I moved out of the neighborhood, so that many of
my old companions couldn't find me, including Rena.

last I heard she went to New York City to study
art.
Frederick's isn't the same without her.

popcorn in the dark

"I remember that night she came over,"
she told me angrily,
"she sat on the floor and
said to you,
'you fucking rotten son-of-a-bitch!'
and you stood over her and said,
'you cheap cunt, you slut, you whore!'
you two really thought you were something,"
she told me.

"look," I told her, "I was working on my
3rd novel and my nerves were raw.
I'd broken out in a rash and my right
arm was going numb.
the clutch on my car had just quit
and I had wax build-up in my ears."

"what's wrong with you now?" she asked.

"insomnia," I said, "lack of purpose,
ingrown toenail, bad luck."

"let's go to a movie," she said.

"anything you want," I said,
throwing the cat off my lap.

when they start talking about the
other woman
it's time for popcorn in the
dark.

a little spot of senseless yellow

you can't tell me it's the best time for poetry,
you can't tell me Marciano couldn't have taken
Louis, you can't tell me that Hitler was a madman, you
can't tell me that dogs bark only at the night;
you can't tell me that the flame doesn't hurt the moth,
you can't tell me that those people there on the corner
standing and blinking their eyes are
human; you can't tell me that love is more than
life, and you can't stretch out on the same mattress with me
and say, "I love you"
because—
we're out of cigarettes and we're out of love and my
battery is low and my bones ache
and Lorca is dead and
Neruda is dead and Christ with hazel eyes
was gaffed like a fish
by little men with dirty fingernails.
we're out of wine and love and luck. and you can't
tell me anything. so why don't you get up and tap that toilet
handle a few times? or it will just keep running like that
forever.

Toulouse

he had an accident as a child
and they had to operate on his legs
and when they were done
his legs grew only about half the length
they were meant to be
and that's the way he reached
manhood.
on those very short legs
he hung around the Paris cafés
and sketched the dancing girls
and the girls in the brothels
and drank too much
(it's strange that most of those
who create well seem to have some sad
malady)
he subsisted on the sale of his paintings
and on loans from his family
and achieved some success
when along came a beautiful
and terrible whore
and he painted her like never before
and they became involved
short legs and all.
she, of course, was hardly faithful,
and one night, defending her
faithlessness
she mocked him and his legs.
that ended the affair.
he turned on the gas jet
then shut it off in order
to finish another painting.

he was always a little gentleman.
he wore a neat suit and
he liked to wear a top hat
while he sketched the turbulent nightlife
around him,
doing that as well as it has ever been done,
cutting through the odds,

somehow getting it down tight and vivid and
clean
as he sketched the whores and dancing
girls
who would never be his,
and finally one night
he finished his last
sketch and then
tumbling drunk down a steep dark
stairway
little legs kicking
he became permanently involved with that
other
final and terrible and beautiful
whore.

Bruckner (2)

Bruckner wasn't bad
even though he got down
on his knees
and proclaimed Wagner
the master.

it saddens me, I guess,
in a small way
because while Wagner was
hitting all those homers
Bruckner was sacrificing
the runners to second
and he knew it.

and I know that
mixing baseball metaphors with classical
music
will not please the purists
either.

I prefer Ruth to most of his teammates
but I appreciate those others who did
the best they could
and kept on doing it
even when they knew they
were second best.

this is your club fighter
your back-up quarterback
the unknown jock who sometimes
brings one in
at 40-to-one.

this was Bruckner.

there are times when we should
remember
the strange courage
of the second-rate

who refuse to quit
when the nights
are black and long and sleepless
and the days are without
end.

in dreams begin responsibilities

he had velvet eyes and trouble with Paul Goodman
and his gang,
he wrote to Pound to illustrate where Ezra
had erred in the *Cantos*.
at 24, a poet-critic, the *Kenyon Review* darling,
one of the *Partisan
Review* darlings, he corresponded with Tate, visited
John Crowe Ransom,
had insomnia, starkly burned, lectured at Princeton,
had problems with his peers and with his wives,
began losing a mental step here and there
and also, of course, he was Jewish and therefore sad.
that first great promise began to develop a tic
under the right eye
and he knew less of women than any high school boy.
he wrote Laughlin of New Directions
about the state of his fame and his manhood;
he began drinking more, taking sleeping pills
and dexies
and like anybody else
he started getting older,
took to living in small rented rooms
and like his ex-friends and lovers
rooted for the Giants.
he began to fatten in face and body,
preferred early photographs of himself
(the altar boy appearance now long gone)
and refused to have a
new portrait taken for his
publisher to use.

then he stopped writing.
although considered a genius by his peers
his books never sold very well
some say because he was too good;
others said something else.

his criticism was brilliant in its
rancor and decisiveness;

he was really more of a bitch than a
bard—
his poetry too fawning and
delicate.
as a critic he was a good surgeon,
as a poet he was stalled in a kind of stale
whimsy.
at any rate
he stopped writing both.

somehow they finally did get him to sit for a photo.
the last photo of him:
sitting on a bench in Washington Square
caught forever
with a strange oblong glance
looking down and to the left.

he died at 44
of a heart attack.
gathering at the same bar
once frequented by
Dylan Thomas,
the latest poets
the new poets
bellied-up
hoping to be struck by
that same miracle,
that same
flash of light
he had enjoyed.

but his was a
grievous life
at best.

uncrowned

a retired middleweight boxer, Hayden Stuhlsatz, fought
under the name Young Stanley, won 102 of 121 fights
between 1929 and 1941.
he fought and beat four men who were middleweight champions
or who would become champions.
he beat reigning middleweight champ Vince Dundee
on June 26, 1934
but since it was a non-title bout
he didn't take the crown.
after that fight he began billing himself as the
"Uncrowned Middleweight Champion of the World."

Stuhlsatz, 68, was struck by a fast-moving
Burlington & Northern freight near an Illinois rail yard.
portions of the fighter's body were discovered
scattered along the track by Elmer Gross
while he was delivering newspapers in downtown
Kewanee.

"I doubt they even knew they hit him,"
said the County Coroner.
an inquest is pending.

what we need

he was an old Beatnik poet
still around
pacing my rug
drinking my beer

that dirty scarf wrapped around his
throat

he dashed into my bathroom
unzipped
pissed
finished
zipped up

flushed
almost breaking the
handle

he examined his
face
in the mirror

came out
saying, "I'm gonna write a
POEM, man! I'm gonna tell 'em
how FUCKED-UP this world is,
man!"

"one of the reasons the world
is fucked-up," I told him, "is
that there are too many poets
and too many poems."

he placed himself before me,
legs spread as if he were on a
sinking ship. he flung out
an arm and yelled,
"TOO MANY POETS? TOO MANY
POEMS? NO! THERE AREN'T

ENOUGH! WE NEED MORE POETS,
MORE POEMS! WE HAVE TO FILL
THE STREETS OF THE WORLD WITH
OUR POEMS!"

the thought of that was too
much for me and I
couldn't respond.

the old Beatnik stalked to the
window, glared
out: "shit, I haven't had a
piece of ass in *two years!*"

"have another beer," I told
him.

he whirled and looked at
me: "hey? what's with *you,*
man? where's your COURAGE?
where's your SPIRIT?"

I didn't reply.

the old Beatnik drained his
beer, smiled a little Brando
smile
then
straightened his scarf

dashed to the bathroom
again
unzipped
took it out
didn't have much
luck
zipped up
examined his face
in the mirror
again

came out: "WE NEED MORE
POETS, MAN! THE WORLD
NEEDS MORE POEMS!"

I got up, went to the kitchen
for another beer.
the refrigerator was nice and
quiet when I opened it and when
I closed it softly
it just went
click

and I uncapped the beer and
took a good hit as he
went on talking in
the other room.

Chatterton took rat poison and
left the rest of us in peace

the old beatnik poet came by once again
with his paintings and poems
carrying them in a paper sack.
he'd been to the racetrack and lost.

"I looked for you," he said.
"I was in the clubhouse," I told him.
"what the hell were you doing in the
clubhouse?" he asked.
"it's air-conditioned and I don't like
my ass to sweat," I replied.

I opened some beer while waiting for
the wine to get cold.
he was a better poet than most but he did
talk LOUD.

"Jesus, baby, hold it down," I
begged.

he was from Brooklyn and he was
very good at expressing himself about
that which didn't suit him.

"you keep writing the same old stuff,"
he told me, "you're getting soft."

"I think I might move out of here,"
I said. "I think I'll move to Malibu."
"hey, man," he said, "I used to know you
when you lived in a tiny room and talked
to the rats and the roaches.
you were writing *great* stuff then..."
"thank you, my man," I answered.

we drank a while and then he started
showing me his paintings.

"not bad, baby," I said.

"now I'm gonna read you some of my poems,"
he said.
"hey, wait a minute," I said, "I mean,
shit, let's just sit and talk."
"no, no, I'm gonna read you my poems,"
he said.

he had the pages in his hand and he
began.

his poems were always the same too.
I wrote about the racetrack and about
women and getting drunk and
he wrote about
the Poets
the Desperate Poets and the Mad Poets and the
Unrecognized Poets
who really did say it best
who got it down better than the others
but nobody cared
the editors and publishers were all
sucks and assholes
they couldn't tell talent from
titty
Olson was shit
Ferlinghetti was shit
Mark Strand was shit
Ginsberg sat in coffee houses and
was a shit;
but the moon knew what was what
and shone down only upon the
True Poets
while the editors and publishers
fucked teeny-boppers
on top of their desks
and nobody cared.
but they'd find out about him
(a True Poet)
after he died and

it didn't matter because
the cocky moon knew
and the beautiful whore knew
the beautiful whore in room eleven
back at the Viking Motel,
that whore with the soul
of an angel
she knew
and the ocean and the stars knew too.

the old beatnik poet launched into another
poem. I had written blurbs for some
of his small press books. it didn't
help. the books didn't sell. I thought that
his poems were better when he stayed away from the
beautiful whores and the moon and the True Poet shit but
his problem was that he was stuck on
the same subject matter
just like the rest of us.
I even liked him for that so long as I didn't have
to see him too often.

we drank and I kept telling him
to lower his voice, he had amazing volume.

anyhow, the old beatnik poet and
I
drank on and on
we drank everything in the place
and there had been plenty there.

I told him he could sleep on the
couch
and he was soon asleep and
he snored the way he talked:
loud.

street poets like him were tough
sons-of-bitches.
I too had been on the streets for
years

but instead of learning grace and
strength
I had only learned terror and insanity
and fear.

as I listened to him snore
I heard a new sound that I knew too
well from living with too many drunks:
he was going to vomit and vomit
plenty.

I got up and placed a wastebasket
by his head.

"what's up? what's zat?" he asked.
"when you puke, let it go in here,"
I told him.
"aw right, aw right..." he answered.
15 minutes later he was at
it.

he was a taco and bean man, a pizza
man, he liked hot dogs. it came
out, plenty of it, and the port wine
and the beer and the double vodka
he'd ordered at the track bar
between the 5th and 6th races when
the beautiful whore with the long legs
standing at the bar
had smiled at him.

it came, plenty of it.

and in the morning he was up at
7:10
walking the rug
talking to himself
and I said, "Jesus Christ, man,
I usually sleep until noon.
what's wrong with you?"
"nothing wrong with me, man,"
he answered, "it's just my *energy!*

besides I usually get up early in
the morning, I got to walk around and
talk to somebody or I know I'm gonna kill
myself."
"o.k.," I said, "go take a walk."
"all right, man," he said, "I'll walk
for an hour so you
can get some sleep."

he left. in 15 minutes he was back, he'd
brought my cat in with him and he was
talking to my cat.

"look, man," I said, "is there some place I can
drive you? is there any place you want to go?"
"yeah," he said, "I'm going to sell a painting
to this guy at 9 a.m. but it's too early yet.
I'll tell ya what. can ya drive me to Westlake
Park?"

I told him that there was no problem.
he gave me 3 of his poems and I gave
him one of my paintings of a whore in long silk
stockings and high heels stretched out on a
couch with her skirt up to her ass.

I did feel that it was considerate of him to get out,
that he had been human enough to recognize
that. we got into the car and I began to
feel bad because in a sense I was
dumping him into a park full of bedraggled
misfits and human hyenas; but I was not a man of broad
conscience; I only wanted my peace and quiet;
and I wanted them more than I wanted him.

as I let the beatnik poet out on
Alvarado Street I looked across and saw the bar
where I had met this woman who had given
me seven years of hell.

he collected his paper sack and stood there alone on the

curb and we made our gang signs and I pulled away,
not my brother's keeper.

I drove home, got there and went back to
sleep.

I got up at noon and made ready for the
track. I got ready to dump the contents of
the wastebasket into the trash bin when I
noticed that he had mostly missed the
target. there were blobs and puddles
on the rug. I was bare-
foot. I lifted one foot, then the
other. I pulled the soft, flattened
pieces off. the stink drifted
up. I pushed the coffee table to one side
and there was more of it. he had attempted
to wipe it up with an old newspaper and
a copy of German *Playboy.*
cleaning up his black brown green
hot dog pizza mustard relish bean gumbo taco
potato chip hamburger-rare-with-onions I felt
abused: they all knock on my door,
I don't knock on their door, never did.

I hope he sells his paintings, I hope his
books sell, I hope he gets to fuck the teeny-
boppers, I hope he gets a big place with German
police dogs and an electric fence, I
hope the angels arrive for him, for him and all
the others; but it isn't going to happen: it's
a hard marketplace and most of them talk away
what they should write down, and most of those
who manage to write it down for a while
can't continue to do it successfully for
long.

now I've soaked two large towels. I've got to
clean up the remainder of my poet friend. that ought
to help keep me humble and pure and writing my own
good stuff.

Jack

Jack with the long hair.
Jack demanding money.
Jack of the big gut.
Jack of the loud, loud voice.
Jack who prances before the ladies.
Jack who thinks he's a genius.
Jack who badmouths the lucky.
Jack getting older and older.
Jack who talks about it but doesn't do it.
Jack who gets away with murder.
Jack who talks of the old days.
Jack who talks and talks.
Jack with his hand out.
Jack who terrorizes the weak.
Jack the embittered.
Jack of the coffee shops.
Jack begging for recognition.
Jack who never had a real job.
Jack who overrates his potential.
Jack who screams about his unrecognized talent.
Jack who blames everybody else.
Jack of all trades.

you know who Jack is.
you saw him yesterday.
you'll see him tomorrow.
you'll see him next week.

wanting it without doing it.
wanting it free.

wanting fame,
wanting women,
wanting everything.

a world full of Jacks
sliding down the
beanstalk.

upon phoning an x-wife not seen for 20 years

I got her number from a friend of mine
she was in Texas and the number rang:
"hello," she said.
"hey, baby," I said, "guess who this is."
"I know who this is," she said.
it was the same icy cultured voice
only now it was crisp with hatred.
"how ya doing?" I asked.
"I'm doing all right," she answered.
"I'm still the same," I said.
"yes," she answered, "I suppose that you are."
"well," I said, "I just wanted to say hello."
she didn't answer.
"well," I said, "lots of luck. goodbye."
"goodbye," she said.
I put the phone down.
well, I thought, that won't be much of a
phone bill.
I walked into the other room and told my
girlfriend: "it's astonishing. she still hates me
after 20 years."
"you bring that out in people," she said.
I walked into the kitchen to inspect my blue Maine
lobster. it was boiling nicely. and now she was
too.

big time loser

I was on the train to Del Mar and I left my seat
to go to the bar car. I had a beer and came
back and sat down.
"pardon me," said the lady next to me, "but you're
sitting in my husband's seat."
"oh yeah?" I said. I picked up my *Racing Form*
and began studying it. the first race looked tough.
then a man was standing there. "hey, buddy,
you're in my seat!"
"I already told him," said the lady, "but he didn't pay
any attention."
"This is *my* seat!" I told the man.
"it's bad enough he takes my seat," said the man
        looking
around, "but now he's reading my *Racing Form*!"
I looked up at him, he was puffing his chest out.
"look at you," I said, "puffing your god-damned
chest out!"
"you're in my seat, buddy!" he told me.
"look," I said, "I've been in this seat since the
train left the station. ask anybody!"
"no, that's not right," said a man behind me,
"*he* had that seat when the train left the
station!"
"are you sure?"
"sure I'm sure!"

I got up and walked to the next train car.
there was my empty seat by the window and there was
my *Racing Form.*

I went back to the other car. the
man was reading his *Racing Form.*
"hey," I started to say ...
"forget it," said the man.
"just leave us alone," said his wife.

I walked back to my car, sat down and
looked out the window

pretending to be interested in the land-
scape,
happy that the people in my car didn't know what
the people in the other car knew.

like a movie

it was like a movie.
I got the phone call and picked her up
at a bar off of
Vine St.
she was waiting in a booth
and the patrons were watching a
baseball game.
Friday evening.
she was drinking white
wine.
I got the tab: $4.75
and left a
quarter tip.

when she saw my 15-year-old car
she said,
shit.

I said, do you want to get in or
not?

she got in.

at my place I rolled her a joint
and poured 2 scotch and
sodas.

she put her head in my lap
and said,
that fucking job is killing
me.

I rubbed her temples, her nose,
her eyebrows. she arched her neck
to kiss me. I kissed
her.

the phone rang. I got up and
answered it, came back, sat

down.

that was Vicki, I said, you've got to
go.

shit, she said from flat on her back,
when do you write?

I smiled at her
as she left
and closed the
door.

an unusual woman

I met this woman
and she said,
you're in terrible shape,
let's clean you up,
and she started squeezing my
blackheads.
she squeezed those blackheads
everywhere:
in the car, in the market, in
bed, in the park
(in between we made
love).
I ran out of blackheads before I
ran out of
love.
what are we doing to do
now? she asked.

then she began plucking hair out
of my ears and nose and from around my eyes
and eyebrows, from my back,
with a tweezer. we ran out of
hair before I
ran out of
love.
what are we going to do
now? she asked.

I ran out of blackheads and hair
before I ran out of
love.
now she's packed her clothes and
is moving out
tonight but not before she
cleans the wax
out of my
ears.

a highly unusual
woman.

pale pink Porsche

she's gotten very fat
since we split a year ago
(but I haven't lost weight either)

and she has her millionaire
who pays the bills
and I have my women that
come and go and then
return

she and I drink and
sleep together
but we no longer
make love

in the mornings I walk her out
to her Porsche

we were never married
yet now we are divorced

I wave goodbye to her
as she drives away

then I go in
fix breakfast
sit down
and type a
four-page love letter
to another lost lady in
Galveston,
Texas.

the arrangement

there's a mannequin in this junk shop,
I tell her, it's for sale, she's really
a class broad, really a class broad,
but I'm ashamed to go in and buy
her. will you buy her for me?

they made a movie once,
she says. this guy falls in love with a
mannequin, they live together, you know,
but it finally goes wrong
and he smashes the body, the arms, the head,
everything.

well, I say, I want this mannequin,
I want you to buy me this mannequin.

I don't want you making love to that thing
more than twice a week. the rest of you
belongs to me.

fine, I say, only look and see if it has
legs, it isn't any good without legs.
lift the skirt and look. sometimes they
just stand up on wires, especially
when they wear long skirts.

all right, she says, I'll look under the
skirt.

I'm getting hot, I say, I've never made love to
a mannequin.

you realize, she says, that this will create a love
triangle?

we'll work it out, I say, we'll work it out
somehow.

do I have to watch while you do it?

only if you want to. and don't forget to look
under the skirt.

I won't. will you empty the garbage while I'm
gone?

yes, my love, I will.

polish sausage

come on, she said, I want you to meet my friends,
it's a lovely drive, I'll drive,
and we went
and she said, look, all this sky, all the
mountains, doesn't it refresh your
soul?

she drove around the curves
she liked to drive around the curves
it went on for hours and then we were
there.

there was a young girl in the yard planting a young
tree.
there was a young man there
too.

we went inside and drank some beer.
there was a parrot with a very yellow
head.
there was a bag of dry cookies.

then the one who had driven me up
went into the bathroom and vomited up her
dry cookies.

afterward she got on the motorcycle with the young man
and they drove off for some more beer and some
polish
sausage.

meanwhile, his girl played me some
redneck music.

she said it was great.

how many minutes we got before they get back?
I asked.
8, she said.

when they got back
there were some jokes about the
local fire department
and some minor brilliancies about nothing in
particular.

we decided that someday we might have a party up there,
no more than
12 people.

on the way back
driving down the mountain
driving down the curves
she said,
you know, you're a very strange
person.

I reached forward to the dash
took a cigarette
lit it.

and the curves went down and around and
around
and I thought
yes, it's true:

there's nothing likeable
about
the trees or the mountain
or the
hours
gone.

I took out a piece of paper
and wrote:
love is a tiny spot
3 quarters of an inch
below the left
tit.

then I felt
better.

down by the sea, the beautiful sea

we were telling stories and
my little girl
said, there was this purple bush
and this purple bush had a beard
just the color of this sand:
red and black and white
like a flag
and there was this yellow bush
and the purple bush began to
grow bananas
and that's very unusual for a bush
to grow bananas
so the yellow bush decided to strangle the
purple bush
because it was
jealous
but the purple bush strangled the yellow bush
first
then a fox full of jelly
got jealous of the purple
bush and he went to the animals in the
forest and they decided to strangle the
purple bush
but they got mixed up and the animals
strangled themselves
and the purple bush kept right on growing
bananas on itself
and then everything came back to life again
the animals in the forest and
even the yellow bush
and they all were friends and
sat around and watched the bananas
grow.

look, I said, that airplane. look how low it looks
over the water. it looks like it's going to fall into
the ocean.

we both sat up and watched the airplane but we couldn't

quite tell if it did
before it vanished behind one of the burned-out
piers.

the guitar player

he came from South Carolina
with his young wife and
two kids
had a new red truck
and a guitar.
he came to Hollywood
to sing.
you know
how it is
when the hometown folks
tell you
how good you are.

he got a job
landscaping
lived in the
front apartment with his
wife and two kids.
I got to know him
went down and
drank with him
listened to him
sing—
not bad
not great
but not
bad
but you know that
the neighborhood
was full of guitars
and singers
not bad or great
but
good.

his name was
Rex
and then Rex
met another guy

who lived in a back
unit
named Del.
Del sold grass
and speed and
sometimes
H.

Rex started to
hang with Del.
I didn't care much
for Del.
he had a mongrel dog
he kept tied
with a rope
and
he beat the dog
too much.

soon Rex
stopped singing
and he
stopped working.
his wife
got a job
cleaning house
for some rich guy
in the hills
and maybe as part
of her job
he gave her one
of his cars to use
and the kids ran
up and down
the sidewalk
in front
and I didn't see
Rex much
anymore.
he just stayed
in his room.

with the shades
pulled down.

I asked his
wife, "is Rex
all right?"

"he's got
sleeping sickness,"
she told me.

well
Rex lucked out.
one day
he
looked around and
put his family
his guitar
and
a few things
into that
red truck
and drove
all the way back
to South Carolina.

soon after that
Del o.d.'d
and they
carried him out
in a
zipped-up
black body bag
an old one
and his
naked feet
stuck out of
the end
as they took him
down the
walkway.

somebody took in
the mongrel
and Rex's wife
wrote us
from S.C.
that Rex was
singing again
he was thinking of
going to Nashville
and he had
a good job
and it
was nice
that
they had known us.
we
were the only
people
in the court
who had
a little flower
and
vegetable garden
in front
of our place.
it made them think
of home
and Rex
says
"hello."

social butterfly

I walked in and took a seat at the end of the counter and
opened my newspaper and the man next to me saw me reading
    about
the 49er-Buccaneer game coming up. "I'd like to see Tampa beat
the 49ers," he said. I told the man that I always liked it when
the 49ers lost but I couldn't see them losing three straight.
then I gave my order to the waitress and turned to the
race results. "I've got a good friend at the track," he said,
"he gives me tips. I'm going to the races Sunday. I've
got a hot top." I told him I was trying to stay away from the
races, that I was fighting to stay away, and then my order
came: a tuna fish sandwich. "you remember 2 or 3 years ago?"
he asked, "they said swordfish had lead in them? or maybe it was
mercury? I catch my own tuna and can it. costs me $7.45
a can to can my tuna. it's a real rip-off." his order came.
"look at that hamburger," he said, "how the hell you gonna get
your mouth around that?" "I'm not," I told him. he got quiet
with the mouthfuls and I turned to the financial page. "the
    market,"
I said before he could, "went up 135 points in one day. how the
hell's a man gonna figure on a thing like that?" "the brokers
don't know," he answered, "the analysts don't know, the investors
don't know, nobody knows..." "somebody must know," I said.
"nobody knows," he said. "I mean," I suggested, "somebody
somewhere must know? one guy, maybe?" "nobody knows," he
said.

he finished his hamburger and picked up the bill. "well,
it was nice talking to you," he said. "sure," I said, "take
it easy."

people like that used to give me nervous fits and depression
for four or five hours afterwards. now I just relax.
it's easy.

the waitress came up: "care for another coffee?" I told her
yes, that would be nice and as she walked away I looked at her
ass as if I was interested. it's best to keep acting, look
normal, hide in the crowd and stay out of sight, and the best

way to hide is to act just like everybody else. she came back with
the coffee. "care for a pie or something?" she asked. I told her,
"no, gotta keep the waistline down." she said, "ah, come on,
you only live once." "o.k.," I said, "I'll take the blueberry
with a scoop of vanilla."

and as she walked away again I stared at her ass and
wondered why.

a fan letter

dear Mr. Chinaski, you probably get many letters
and I guess you hardly ever bother to read them
but shit, man, it would really be good to get
an answer from old Chinaski, you know, to find it there
in the mailbox when I come home from the foundry
where I work as a grinder-chipper.
my girlfriend just left me, man, after 6 years,
just like that.
well, I'll just kick back and read Kerouac.
did you ever meet Kerouac?
you know, you try to come off as a tough old
cat but I bet you're soft, man, soft as slime.
I'm 25 and I've been writing 9 years and the
stuff keeps coming back.
I do jazz-poetry readings at the local bar
and they seem to like it; I mean, there are always some
shits who don't understand anything.
do you write in the morning or do you write
at night?
and what's with the racetrack, man?
I mean, every time I go to the track I come back
with shit and no toilet paper.
enclosed is some poetry but you don't have to
read it.

you know, most of your stuff is just boring impressions
of two-bit burnt-out mental
fucks.
how can you possibly drink while you write?

well, you don't have to answer this letter and
you can tear up the fucking poems.
forget I sent them.
forget I wrote them.

I'm just going to crawl into the fucking
bathtub and ruminate.

    yrs.,

    Billy (Chips) Weatherton

I'm a failure

I locked my car door
and this
guy walked up
he looked like my old
friend Peter
but it wasn't Peter
it was a skinny dude
in blue workshirt and torn jeans
and he said,
"hey, man, my wife and I
need something to eat!
we're starving!"
I looked behind him
and there was his
woman
and she stared at me
her eyes brimming with
tears.
I gave him a five.
"I *love* you, man!" he
hollered, "and I'm not going to
spend it on booze!"
"why not?" I said.

I went and
took care of some business
came back
got into my car
and
contemplated
whether I had done
something good
or been taken.

as I drove off
I remembered my years on the
bum
starved damn near beyond repair and
I had never asked anyone for a

dime.

that night
I explained to the lady I lived with
how I often gave money to panhandlers
but that
in the darkest hungriest times of my
life I had refused
to ask anyone for
anything.

"you just never knew how to do any-
thing right," she said.

too dark

"no," she said, "I know you fucked another woman
in our bed while I was in Arizona and I will not
sleep with you in that bed."
"but look, Baby," I said, "I live here, and I know
you also got some in Arizona."
"I don't care," she said, "I will not sleep with you
in that bed."
"well," I asked, "how about your place? I don't mind
even if you have..."
"no," she said, "we've got to go to a motel."
"all right," I said, "let's go..."

so we drove around and found a motel called
BILLY'S DREAM VILLAGE
and I gave the man 30 dollars
and we went down to #17
got ready for bed
got in
turned out the lights.

it was totally dark
never had I ever experienced such a total
DARK.

"it's too dark," I said,
"I feel as if we are buried alive.
I can't do it here..."

"I can't do it here either," she said.

"we can try," I said.

"no, I can't even try,"
she said.

we got dressed and I drove her
back to her place.

"I'll phone you in the morning,"

she said.

I drove back to my place, undressed,
cut the light and went to
bed.

then I remembered that I hadn't brushed
my teeth.

fuck it, I thought, fuck my teeth.

I lay there a while.

then I got up and brushed my
teeth.

this is a fact

in the company of fools
we relax upon
ordinary embankments,
enjoy bad food, cheap
drink,
mingle with the men and
ladies from
hell.
in the company of fools
we throw days away like
paper napkins.

in this company
our music is loud and our
laughter
untrue.

we have nothing to lose
but our selves.

join us.
we are now
almost
the entire
world.

God bless
us.

there's one in every bar

the pathetic squirrel drinks Johnny Walker Red
at Stinky's Bar & Grill.
in love with the cocktail waitress
he watches her body
her eyes
he dreams of her on his sofa
crossing her legs and giggling
he dreams of her drunk in his bedroom
he dreams of victory
of conquest
he leaves her very large tips
he says very little to her.
the pathetic squirrel dislikes
how crude and obvious the other
bar-squirrels are
to her
and he's delighted when
she laughs at them
and says things like
"back off, Marty!"
the pathetic squirrel loves the large bow
on the back of her short dress.

he leaves each night
intoxicated
knowing he will be sick on the job
the next day.

the pathetic squirrel is in love with the
cocktail waitress
but ask her about him
and she'll confide:
"he makes me sick! he's a complete asshole!"

and she's right.
but he still has his dream
and that might be enough in itself
because he doesn't realize that
she's a complete asshole
too.

the beautiful rush

I lost a dollar at the track today and I know that's
stupid: it's better to win $500 or lose $500—
there is at least the rush of emotion—
but I was 29 bucks ahead going into the last race so I
laid 30-win on this 8-to-one shot at the end and he
came in second, it was too bad,
that's all. so
I lost a dollar.

but sometimes we've got to settle for not much;
we need our rest; the great tragedy or the great victory will
arrive soon enough.

so I sit here tonight listening to
a Vaughan Williams symphony on the radio and you
too are probably sitting and waiting for something better
or worse to come.
waiting is the greater portion of being alive.

I waited on that 8-to-one shot in the last race and
he came on in the stretch rapidly closing the space
between himself and the other horse at the wire, he came
with a beautiful rush, pounding and driving, to fall a
head short.

such is the life of a gambler: to leave and then wait only
to return.

not all of us are gamblers and those who aren't don't
matter.

over-population

I'll say one thing: her older sister wrote
more novels than anybody I ever knew. she'd
send them to New York but
the novels kept coming back. I read some
of them, or rather, parts of them. maybe
they were good, I don't know. I'm not a
critic and I don't like Tolstoy or Thomas
Mann or Henry James.
anyhow, her novels kept coming back and her
men kept leaving. she just ate more and more,
had more babies; she didn't bathe and seldom
combed her hair and she'd let the many soiled diapers
lie about. she talked and laughed
continually—a highly nervous and
irritating laugh. her endless talk was all about men and sex
and I never interrupted her be-
cause I sensed she had enough troubles and besides
I was living with her younger sister.

but one afternoon when we were visiting, the
older sister said to me: "all right, I know
you've had some novels published but I have
my babies, my children, that's art,
that's *my* art!"

"many people have babies," I said, "that's
really not exceptional,
but to write a good novel is a rare and
exceptional thing."

she leaped up and waved her arms: "oh yeah?
oh yeah? what about *your* daughter? where
is *your* daughter now?"

"Santa Monica, California."

"*Santa Monica? what the hell kind of father
are you?*"

I no longer see either sister, although
about 2 months ago the younger one phoned
long distance and among other things she
told me that her sister had just mailed
her latest novel off to New York and that
they all thought it was very good, that
it certainly was the one, that is was the one that
would finally do it for her.

I didn't tell her younger sister that
all of us novelists think like that and that's
why there are so many of us.

an old love

now her hair is white
she's only in her mid-40s
still lives in my neighborhood.
a couple of years ago
the first time I saw her she screamed:
"you old fucker! I know you're fucking
all those young girls! you ought to be
ashamed of yourself!"

next time I saw her
a week later
she told me:
"you know, 2 homeless raped a girl
last night—right down the street. but
they caught them! they caught those dirty
bastards!"

the next time I saw her she was watching a
young man in a car making a
U-turn. as his car passed her she
screamed: "you ain't gonna pick up
my ass, punk!
I'm going to report you to the cops!"

my new girlfriend came to
see me recently. "my god!" she said.
"my god!"

"what?"

"who's the woman with the
white hair and bobby sox
and the dirty white dog?"

"oh, she lives in the grey bungalow
down the street..."

"she said I was an eater of shit
a prostitute and a

bitch!"

"she did?"

"she almost attacked me! her
dog growled!"

"she's crazy, I guess."

we sat down across from each other
at the coffeetable and I opened a
bottle of good white wine.

"I know *you'd* never go to bed with someone like
that!" she said.

"yeah, she's something else," I said and poured 2
glasses full.

beds, bathrooms, you and me

think of all the beds
everywhere
used again and again
to love in
to sleep in
to die in.

and all the bathrooms
used again and again
to bathe in
sometimes to love in.

in this land
some of us love better than
we die
but most of us die
better than we
love
and we die
piece by piece
bit by bit
in parks
eating ice cream, or
in igloos
equipped with refrigerators,
of dementia,
or on straw mats
or upon disemboweled
loves
or
or...

beds beds beds
bathrooms bathrooms bathrooms

the human sleeping systems
the human bathing systems
are the world's greatest
inventions.

but we couldn't leave well
enough alone.
you re-invented me
and I re-invented you
and that's why we don't
get along on
this bed
or in our bathroom
any longer.

puzzle

I was driving on the freeway
listening to the radio
when the newscaster announced
that a car had crashed through
a guard rail and
down into a body of water
and the occupant was apparently
drowned.

then there was a taped
conversation with a police
official:
"I don't really understand
this one. I don't see how
she could have driven through
that heavy rail. the visibility
was perfect. the doors were locked and
the windows were
up which indicates
that she was alone. this one
really puzzles me..."

I didn't understand why the
doors and windows told
him that she was alone:
possibly something he learned at
the Police Academy?

anyhow
I have a favorite spot
picked out
down near Del Mar.
the railing looks weak and
there's an 80-foot drop
straight down the cliff
and
into the ocean.
I may never use it
but it's nice to know

that it's there.

(I intend to have a 5th
of whiskey at my lips,
the radio playing classical
music
and I will break through
that railing
fast
launching the car
high up
over the water...)

the radio then informed me that
the driver was
in her early twenties—
name being withheld until
notification of her next of
kin.

I switched stations then
to where a man was
singing, "*I told the
daffodils that
at last
my heart's an
open book...*"

the traffic was bad
too.

hot dog

almost every time
after we started in
here he would come
this big black hairy
male hound
dripping of mouth
stinking
panting
lurid
whimpering
begging
snorting through wet
nostrils
he stank like a Hollywood motel
doormat
wet in the rain

and when I stopped to kick
him off the bed
she'd say:
"oh! please don't hurt Timmy!"

and Timmy would run in neurotic
circles
smelling his
asshole
and I'd return to my task
and begin to near completion
when Timmy would bound up on the bed
once again.

being in the missionary position
I was able to rap him
a good one or two
across the snout
but that didn't stop him
from
sniffing
drooling

poking
and that's the way we'd
finish—
all three of
us.

she had a good job down on
Sunset Boulevard
(which was more than I could
say)
and when she left in the
morning
she'd tell me
to go out the back way
because mother had an apartment
up front
and she didn't want her mom
to see me.

then I'd
look at that dog
and his eyes would look up
sadly into mine.
we had no
secrets.
I knew and he knew
that we were both
her lovers.

and I also knew looking
at him that
he needed her more than
I did.

I left that last morning
driving in the bright
sunshine
feeling
lost
spooked
unreal

but still
all right.

she phoned me 3 or 4 times
after that.
but I knew it was over.
done.

because when I looked into his brown
eyes
that last morning
I knew
he loved her
more than I did.

maybe if Timmy had been
a man
I wouldn't have
given her up.

but then
I never met a man
with eyes as beautiful
as those on that dog.

the fall

there's a preacher on a UHF channel
I really enjoy.
let's call him Joe Warts.
he runs a talk show
wherein he invites hated
guests.
and behind Joe Warts is
an American flag and a photo of
John Wayne
and in his audience are these bulky
white boys
between the ages of 17 and 30
and they love
Joe Warts
because Joe Warts believes in
America and God.

so these kids from Glendale,
Burbank and like places
scream
wave their arms
as Joe
attacks his guests:
"hey, faggot, you live in a
commune, right? you got those people
brain-washed, right?
admit it, faggot, you grow your own
GRASS up in those hills,
right?
*you people live on relief which comes
out of our taxes!
we work to support you and you lay up there
smoking POT! I'll tell ya what we're
going to do, faggot! we're going to take up a
collection and send the whole gang of you dead-
beats to Red China!*

the guys in the audience go wild, wild!

Joe Warts is good, he can scream good
and he handpicks his guests,
he wins night after night.
the only time he ever made a
mistake
was the night he invited two
female mud wrestlers
on his show.

when the ladies came out
to take their seats
the bulky lads started
whistling and
yowling.
Joe admonished his gang to
"settle down."
then he turned to his
guests and
screamed at them
that
who would want to watch a
couple of women wrestle each other
in the mud?
and,
why did they go around half-
clad like that?
it was disgusting in his eyes *and*
in the eyes of the
Lord!

both girls just
giggled and wiggled in their seats and
said
that other women wore less every day
on the beach.
and also,
lots of men came to see them
wrestle in the mud, in fact, every
night was standing room only.
and they also wrestled in
oil

and the pay was good,
it sure beat being a
waitress or a secretary or a
prostitute,
and they had nothing against
America or God
but they'd mud wrestle or oil
wrestle in
Russia or China or France or
anywhere else
and that
if he didn't shut up
they both
would pin his ass
to the wall
right then and there!

the guys jumped up and screamed and
waved and yowled
but finally not for
Joe Warts
who sat
open-mouthed and silent
as behind him
the photo of John Wayne
blushed.

on bums and heroes

I've thought about e. e. cummings sitting on his front
porch thinking about nothing
or Thurber going blind
and writing upper middle class stories of madness.
now a few miles east of here
the Queen Mary sits moored in Long Beach Harbor
motionless
with tourists in deck chairs
dreaming of how it used to be,
paying to do that
while the Queen Mary
falls millions of dollars into debt
and nobody knows what to do with
her.

the chances get less and less.
the man who used to live here
I still get his magazines and advertisements:
toy soldiers and tanks
that can move and shoot;
World War I uniforms, medals, helmets,
guns;
mace cans, weapons of all sorts;
long knives more beautiful than
the legs of women.

I think of Tolstoy going mad
giving it all away to God and the peasants
and the peasants took it all:
his house, his rubles, everything.
this Spiritual Communism
was necessary to Leo.
then he sat by the side of the road
satisfied and at peace
and after that
he wrote nothing but crap.

Hemingway typed standing up
usually beginning at 6 a.m.

one of his definitions of an
alcoholic was
someone who drank before
noon.
Ernest seldom wrote anything in the
afternoon.

there was a cricket who
crawled into an opening in the wall
downstairs
where an electric socket used to
be
and it was pleasant
because when I turned out the lights
at night
the crickets outside
would begin their music
and his music would come from
inside the wall.
"let's save him," she said,
"he's going to starve."
"yes," I said
getting up and looking into the
hole
but he always got quiet when I
got close.
then one night
you know the rest.
the chances get less and less.

when I was very young
about 17
I'd never heard Sibelius or
Shostakovitch
there was no one for me
except this man in his mid-
thirties
who played right field
for the Angels
in the old Pacific Coast League
batted left-handed

never made the majors
but hit .332, .338, .337
year after year.
it was something about
the way he stood at the plate
calmly
effortlessly
and with style.
one doesn't forget
first heroes.
two or three years ago
I saw the obit
3 lines in an L.A. daily:
he'd died at
75.
atta boy, Cleo.

Big Sam
he was so big standing there
at Sunset and Western.
he walked through clouds and walls.
"I can see it's going to be a
beautiful day!" he'd say.
he talked to cops and old
ladies
was always sucking on a cigar
and grinning,
he knew every prostitute within
five miles.
"I can fix you up with anything
you want, Hank, free..."
then it began to happen,
he got thinner
and thinner
he stopped grinning
started gambling in Las Vegas
20 hours a day
not coming back to his place
sleeping in a public crapper
for 4 hours
then back to the tables.

then he vanished.
it took me two weeks to locate
him
in an old apartment building on
South Normandie Avenue
he was sitting over a dishpan
among empty milk cartons
with this sour smell
everywhere
and those eyes
close to weeping
but not weeping.
"it's good to see you, Hank,"
he said.
the doctors
had told him that
there was something terribly wrong.
Sam, I don't like the way it
happens.
sometimes it happens too fast
sometimes it happens too slow.
I never thought it would happen to you,
Sam,
but I can see you're getting
ready.

the chances get less and less.

3

the soulless life

running on empty

do you see
the tired plants?
the tramp steamers and smiling whores?
the plastic masks of glory?
France and the warm earth?
the high hours?

do you see
now that you see that
everything they told us
was wrong?

the elephant caught
like that
and caged
like that?

the way they tricked us
and caged us too?

how sweetly sad it seems
how sad and sweet
passing lonely people on
the street
the skulls beneath
the skin
the arteries bravely
pumping liquid
as they rush to do
all the foolish things that
they must do.

but what you don't see
is this clock that says
midnight
and this heart in my
self
running on empty.

what you do see is that
what mattered most
doesn't matter so much
anymore.

what you do see is
the dog on the freeway
that doesn't move.

what you do see are
frightened men in tanks and uniforms
not unlike the factory hands
I once knew.

what you do see is
Toulouse-Lautrec pissing
red
and poor Van Gogh
dripping yellow.

what you do see are
frogs and dandelions
dead sparrows in the road
lovers lost in the rain
the hangman swinging in the wind.

now you see.

this habit

it's done by living through the women
and finally without them;
it's done standing by the window
and watching a small dog walk past;
it's done in a café while reading the
race results and eating a sandwich;
it's done while talking to your daughter
who is now a grown woman in college;
it's done while weeding the garden as
you recover from the mess of yesterday;
later the words come, the god-damned lovely
words come again and again
as you sit alone and
type.

"I can hear you typing at night," says
my neighbor.

"oh, I'm sorry..."

"no," he says, "it's a pleasant sound."

he's right, it is.
and when I don't make that sound for
two or three days
I become fretful
my face has an unhealthy hue, and—
you must believe me—
I have visions of
my death.

but when typing I'm
immortal.

well, maybe not immortal.
but this habit
this old typewriter and
this old man
live well together.

madness?

look, he said, admit it.

what? I asked.

when you see that fat woman
in the supermarket who is
picking at the oranges, don't
you feel like going over and
squeezing those ugly haunches
hard
just to hear her scream?

what the hell you talking about,
buddy? I asked.

or when the waiter brings you
your dinner, don't you consider
for a moment that you might
kill him?

not before dinner, I answered.

what I am trying to say here,
he went on,
is that there is a very fine line
between what we call sanity and
what we call madness
and that the effort we make to
stay on the sane side
is only made so that we will
not be punished by
society.
otherwise, we would
often cross that line and
things would be much more
interesting.

I don't know what the hell
you're talking about, buddy,

I told him.

he just sighed, looked at me
and said, forget it, friend.

it's difficult when bananas eat monkeys

it's partly the burning and it's partly the muddy
water and partly the voices—
(the faces I've adjusted to; the years have given
me something)
but when the faces
speak
it makes no pleasure to linger in the crowd.

maybe the truly original man doesn't exist. I
have never met him.

sometimes I think it will be the parking lot attendant. he
walks toward me. he smiles. ah, here it comes, I
think.

then he says, "hi sport," or something else equally flat and
dumb.

I reply with a sentence that sails over his
left shoulder and flames out
on a green balcony across the
street.

I give him my keys
I give him my car

he drives off and I walk into the
place.

the hostess walks
up. "yes?" she
says.

yes, what? I've got to eat so I can
live. I follow her buttocks
(they have a certain minor charm) but I keep
thinking
I've got to tip that son-of-a-bitch out there
when he should be
guillotined.

old man with a cane

I was walking to
the betting window when I heard loud voices coming
from the stairwell near the bar.
a young man was screaming at an old guy with a
cane who had just passed where he sat
on the stairway.

"you farted in my face, you old fuck!"

the old man turned around, pointed his cane
at the young man:

"up your ass!"

I stopped and watched. a whole row of drinkers
at the bar and the bartender watched too.

"you old fuck!" screamed the young man, "I'll
kick your ass!"

"looks to me," said the old man, "like you're
afraid to stand up on your feet and try."

"I'll kick your ass!" screamed the young man,
"you think I won't kick your ass?"

"bullshit," said the old man.
then he turned and slowly walked off.

I watched him leave.
then as I passed the bar
one of the patrons smiled at me:

"that old man either was drunk or he's pretty brave!"

"yeah," said another patron, "that old man
was a tough old bird!"

"I wouldn't want to mess with him!"

said a third.

as I moved off I looked at the row of men
sitting at the bar where they had remained
without moving during the argument.
and the young man still sat on the
steps thinking about the fart and maybe a few
other things.

some days are much more interesting
than others.

empty goblet

she said to me:
"you got drunk and told mother
she had a head like a
cantaloupe."

she continued:
"well, your head doesn't look
like much either."

"I know," I said.

"you know," she said,
"Marty never meant that much to
me
but he *is* a friend and mother
likes him and he has a
beautiful garden;
he's traveled, cultured and a
gourmet.
he was slaving in the kitchen preparing
our dinner and
what do you do?
you get drunk and keep
hollering 'counsellor, counsellor,
my goblet is empty!' "

"he was always out of the room."

"he was the chef. he takes great pride in his
preparation."

"well, shit, you know, food doesn't mean that
much to me."

"but there are *other* people to consider."

"that's why I should never go to dinner parties."

"but you needn't have attacked mother."

"I was all right for the first couple of hours.
the third hour got to me."

"Marty said later, 'why does he attack your
mother? why doesn't he attack *me*?' "

"he was never in the room."

"you should apologize to mother."

"she's a killer."

"that's what my sister thinks and you don't
like my sister!"

"your sister has a head like a yellow
squash."

now she runs out of the room. she is
angry. I will punish her by not
attending her next dinner party.

and Marty is a good boy but he sucks up too much
and pours much too slow.

an interview

are you getting mellow? he asked.

yes, I said.

do you re-write your poems?

yes.

did you used to re-write?

no.

do you try to stick to a simple form?

yes.

don't you think that something is lost in
re-writing, that something is lost in
sticking to a simple form?

yes, I do.

do you think you'll be able to continue to write well
in this big house?

yes.

have you stopped running with all those crazy
women?

yes.

what will you write about now?

one woman, and other things.

but you've created a different image of yourself.

have I?

yes. how was Paris?

large, filled with gas fumes and people.

do you have friends?

there's a doctor, a lawyer, a publisher and a *maître d'*.

it's not like it used to be.

what do you mean?

I mean, you used to run with interesting bums.

relax, those guys are all bums.

now you have 3 bathrooms.

yes, I piss in one, bathe in the other, shit in the
third.

but don't you fear...?

yes, I always have.

why did you take on such a large mortgage payment?

it's a tax write-off.

you once wrote that all a man needed was what he could carry
in one suitcase.

I still think that's true.

do you think you're getting old?

yes.

are you writing as well as you once did?

better.

how can that be?

believe me, I don't understand it either.

do you have any advice for young writers?

get old.

do you have any advice for older writers?

yes, never believe anything you wrote
yesterday was good enough.

what do you consider important?

having time in which to do nothing at
all and having the desire to do just that.

why do you drink so much?

I don't know.

have you ever analyzed it?

no, I'm afraid I'd start worrying about my god-damned
liver.

what will you do when you can't write as well anymore?

fuck.

I mean, really.

well, like most writers,
I won't believe it.

who is the worst writer you've ever read?

well, there are two of them.

who?

George Bernard Shaw and W. Somerset Maugham.

why are they so bad?

just bad for me, you understand.

but why?

just a gut reaction.

you're being kind.

I'm a kind person.

many of your readers don't think so.

what do *you* think?

I think you're getting tired now.

fatigue helps one to be kind. do you think I'm
finished?

I'll know when I read your next book.

how will I know when you're finished?

I don't pretend to be a writer.

what do you pretend to be?

your interviewer.

well, you're a fairly good one. when will you be
finished with me?

I think we're both finished now, he said,
turning off the tape machine.

poem, poem, poem, poem

fellow I know,
(I know him well, it's me)
many of his poems are about writing
poems.
it's easy, it's like making a grocery
list:
I haven't written a poem in 3
weeks.
today I wrote a poem.
she came by and I read her the
poem
but she wanted drugs.
I sat and typed while she
complained.
I put on the record player and kept
typing.
she called me selfish,
slammed the door and
left.
I got up and fed the fish and
boiled an
egg.
then I came back, ripped
the sheet out of the typer
and then I wrote
this.
a poem.
that's all there
is
now.
this poem.
she's gone.
she's mad.
she wanted drugs.
she called me
selfish.
fuck her.

the soulless life

I meet the movie star, he's playing Chinaski
in my new movie, I put my hand on his shoulder: "you're
all right, Ben," I tell him.
then the famous Italian director puts his leg up on
the table: "now I'll drink with you Chinaski," he says.
(that's the way he always drinks, I'm told.)
"o.k.," I say and I put *my* leg up on the table.
I drain my glass, he fills it again, I drain it
again, he fills it again.
they know that I am a real guy then.

the next day two Frenchmen and two Italians from the
film crew come over to my place. they think meeting
me has something to do with making the movie better.
one of the Italians, the one snapping me with his
camera, invites me to his place in Italy. his wife
would like to meet me and they have one thousand bottles
of wine in the cellar.
I ask him to write down his address.
we drink all day and into the night.
the next day they all fly back to Italy to finish shooting
and I get some rest.

but not for long: a day or two later Bo Walberg phones,
he's a San Francisco literary hood, he says he's written
an article about me for a men's mag and would I mind going
to someone's studio
near Sunset and Vine for some photos and I say, "all
right."
they put a little girl with big tits in my lap, she
is dressed in black bra and panties, long stockings, high heels,
she scared me, she scares me, and a very sensitive boy
with red hair takes the shots.
of course, we get drunk after all that and somebody puts
some music on and I do an Indian dance for 22 minutes.
they get some good shots, I'm told.

next the great French director knocks at my door.
he is a gloomy little fellow and sits in a dark corner

drinking wine and not saying anything.
I don't feel like talking either, so we sit
a long time not saying much.
then he hands me a big bundle of francs.
he still doesn't talk. he has
a friend with him, another French director and finally
he says to me: "G. wants to use some of your dialogue in
his next film but he says he can't give you screen credit."
"tell him," I say, holding the francs, "that's fine."
I walk upstairs, throw the bundle of francs in a closet,
then come down to sit some more.

next comes a young actor just getting
famous, just missed the Acad Award and he is
really good—at acting—but
he has a rich dull friend with him and they just
sit around and talk about pussy and fucking, maybe
that's what they think I want to
hear.
the boy actor challenges me to a fight.
he's a good actor, he just needs other people's
lines in order to exist.
like mine.

then comes the famous songwriter
who often stays at the Playboy Mansion.
he has written dozens of hit songs that have made
many singers famous.
he's a fuckin' genius and besides that he's a
good guy
but he doesn't drink much
and when they don't drink much they are
hard to talk to.

then the famous folk singer arrives who claims I
have influenced much of his work.
he has just gotten married and his wife is with him
and his wife talks all night and the famous folk
singer just sits and looks down at his shoes.
after many hours she gets tired and they
leave.

I've left lots out, of course, because
all of this has come very late and very suddenly to me
and I don't understand any of it yet. later I meet a
famous German stage director who has pistol duels with
his girlfriend, they shoot at each other continually
I'm told, and they are both very good at it.
I meet him at a bar before a private production of
his latest drama. I catch him glancing at me
over his vodka-and-orange and I ask, "how the hell
do *you* make it?" and he answers, "well, I blush to
the very toes in my shoes to say it but I make plays."
"that figures," I tell him.

I think the problem is
when you meet famous people they don't seem
like much. it's a
very curious thing.
it's like when I was in and out of jail
I looked around at all the guys and I thought,
these guys don't look like jailbirds. where are
the vicious ones? where are the killers?
none of them looked the part.

I suspect that some famous people don't accomplish very
        much:
when you examine their work carefully
it seems curiously weak—
just something taking up space because nothing
else is taking up that particular space
at that particular moment.
I suspect the famous are created mostly by the
audience
and that if I was the only audience
nobody would be
famous.

now I'm just going to sit and listen to the
radio.
why don't you do the
same?

the x-con

he did his time, came out, put on a black outfit and sang
country and western. he had a good deep easy voice, at first
he sang about killing, how good it felt to kill:
there was one song where the son killed the father
(like Dostoyevsky said, who doesn't want to?):
but mostly the songs were about common
people and their hard, everyday lives.
he also liked going back to the prison and singing
for the cons, and they liked it at first, then his
songs began to sound as if somebody else was
writing them, they became less dangerous,
and one night he appeared on a tv special
with dancing girls and Las Vegas comedians, and that
was the night I wrote him off.

after that he continued to go back to sing at the
prisons, but his voice didn't sound as
good anymore, the cons didn't react like they used
to, record sales fell off, and he more or
less vanished for a while, it was said he went from
drink to drugs and then he came back again as a
Born-Again Christian and sales picked up a little,
then fell off again.

I was at the County Fairgrounds today and after the
eleventh race they announced that he'd be singing
at the track that night at 7:30.

when I walked outside I saw the crowd lined up
to buy tickets—not a man or woman in that
crowd, although they had hands and feet and heads,
and shoes on their feet, and they were decently clothed,
there was nobody in that crowd, nothing or nobody at
all.

the way it is now

I'll tell you
I've lived with some gorgeous women
and I was so bewitched by those
beautiful creatures that
my eyebrows twitched.

but I'd rather drive to New York
backwards
than to live with any of them
again.

the next classic stupidity
will be the history
of those fellows
who inherit my female
legacies.

in their case
as in mine
they will find
that madness
is caused by not
being often enough
alone.

dead dog

Larry was subnormal. I always
liked talking to him.

we would stand out in the
smoggy Hollywood street
discussing
matters.

there is a large portion of
myself that has always felt comfortable
with subnormals

so we had a
connection.

on this particular day
he told me, "my dog got
killed so I got another one.
my first dog's name was
Larry. so I named this dog
Larry too."

"that's good, kid," I
told him.

"how ya doin'?" he
asked.

"oh, all right," I
said.

"REALLY?" he
screamed.

he would begin screaming
now and then.
it was very strange.
as strange as naming his
dogs after himself.

"well, not really," I
said. "I haven't had any
dogs killed but my luck hasn't
been too good lately."

"WHAT DO YOU MEAN?" he
screamed.

"it's the woman I'm living
with, Larry. she steals my
money and fucks other
men."

"SHE DOES?"

"keep it *down,* Larry, half the
neighborhood knows about her
already."

"YOU MEAN THE ONE WITH..."

"*quiet,* Larry..."

he moved closer and asked
softly, "you mean the one with
the long red hair and the big
tits?"

"yes, Larry..."

he moved still
closer: "why don't you get
rid of her?"

"I'm working on it,
Larry..."

"do you want to meet my
new dog?"

"maybe tomorrow, Larry, thanks,

and take it easy..."

I walked back to my apartment
and up the walk.
I knew when I opened the door
she would say, "why don't we go and
score some coke?"

she fooled me, she said,
"why do you talk to that
fucking asshole Larry?"

"he's the only one who
understands me," I
answered.

"great," she said. "now
why don't we go out and score
some coke?"

20 bucks

he was famous in his time,
still picks up parts here and there
in the movies and tv.
for years I've seen him at the
racetrack every day.
we never say much.
the way I know he's there, he'll
yell out my name:
"HEY, CHINASKI!"
it'll be on the escalator
or he'll be behind me
or we'll be passing,
"HEY, CHINASKI!"
I'll holler back his name
and that will be it.
years of this.
he knows somebody I know.
that, I suppose, makes the
link.

finally, one day, he came up
to me.
it was after the 5th race.
he saw me coming from the
payoff window with a roll of
money.

"I'm tapped out," he said,
"you holding anything?"

I peeled off a 20 and handed
it to him.

"thanks," he said, "I'll pay you
back tomorrow."

he walked off.

I saw him after the 6th race,

he was walking along a wall
in a shadow.

I turned away and went about
my business.

the next day I didn't see
him.

in fact, 3 months have gone
by and I haven't seen
him.

a lousy 20 bucks
and he's in hiding.

I know he's at the track.
he's ducking and
running.

I wonder how many people
that poor guy is
hiding from?

a lousy 20 bucks.

he used to be famous.
must have had at least a
million.

he just can't pick a
horse.

all his luck came
early.

now
he's hiding.

a lost soul

well, they warned me it would happen.
the phone rings.
I have just finished eating a grapefruit.
there are 3 telephones.
I pick up the one in the breakfast nook.
I am the man from the factories.
I am the one who slept on park benches.
I am the one who tried suicide and failed.
I am the one who lived with a dozen whores.
I am the one who has been in a dozen drunk tanks.
I am the one accused of rape
and the one accused of dodging the draft
when it was not the popular thing to do.
I pick up the phone: "yeh?"
"Chinaski?" he asks.
"yeh?"
it is the editor of one of the leading literary mags
of our great nation.
"listen, we want you to write us a short story.
we haven't heard from you in a long time. what have
you been doing?"
I bite into a piece of well-buttered toast, then
talk as best as I can with my mouth full.
"novel, horses, drinking. yeh."
he answers: "well, send us something soon, will
you?"
I say "yeh." let the phone fall back into the cradle.

now I've got to dream up some bullshit
fantasy to make the people happy.
it doesn't please me.

I open a couple of cans of cat food and feed the cats.
there are two of them.
one will only eat tuna.
the other just beef and hearts.
hardly park bench factory cats.
I look at them, fat and satisfied.
they bend over their dishes and show me their

dry bungholes.
well, shit, now will I go to the racetrack or
will I rip off a quick story for one grand?

on the freeway I open the sunroof and my writer's
locks blow in the 65 mph Calif. wind.
I can write the story tonight, meanwhile I can
check the whores at the racetrack
bar, they are all wearing slit skirts now,
slit right to the hip, some wear panties, the best
do not.

wheeling down Century Blvd. listening to Mahler
I figure I'm not the worst of the crowd.
today I read in the newspaper about a pop star
who turned up at the
International Whaling Commission with his guitar and
presented a petition signed by a half-million Americans
calling for an end to whaling. then he sang a song titled,
"I Want to Live."
the I.W.C. did not seem to be impressed.
later the singer told a reporter:
"I have swum with whales and they
are wonderful friendly creatures, as interested in me
as I am in them. I came here as a human being who
        celebrates
life on this planet and I hope to share my life and my songs
with all other creatures that live and breathe."

I am almost at the track.
I pull in, go to valet parking.
all the attendants know me.
one of them hands me my parking tab.
asks: "how ya doin', champ?"
I grunt, give him a nod, climb out,
jerk my right shoulder just so,
glance to the left and
move off to the clubhouse.

compassion

she comes in and tells me that she just saw a dog
run over, only the wheels didn't crush him, the car
passed over him and he ran off dazed and limping,
no dog collar, very thin, starved.
she says we ought to go find him and I say she ought
to call the dog pound
and she says that they will only kill him later
if she does.

that evening we go to dinner and as we are driving back
we pass a station wagon with some boys in the back and she
says,
"did you see that?" there was a little
boy tied up and screaming in the back
of that car!"
I laugh and she asks, "what are you laughing at?"
"it's only kids playing," I say, "cowboys and Indians, Batman
or whatever they're into now. used to happen to me often,
they always tied me up."
"please drive back," she says, "let's make sure nothing is
wrong!"
I laugh again.

we stop for a traffic light and I notice that the paint
on the hood is looking dull—I'm going to have to get a
wax job soon.
she stares straight ahead and doesn't speak.
as the light turns green
I turn up the music on the radio real
loud.

he also flosses every day

The Strangler has
murdered and sexually molested
eleven young women in the
Los Angeles and Hollywood
area.

it is now 5 days until Christmas
for him
just like it is for the rest of
us.

there is a special 65-man
Strangler Task Force at work
night and day.

most of the girls were
prostitutes.

everywhere you go
people talk about The
Strangler.

they talk about him at
the Sizzler
at McDonald's
at the Pussycat Theater
at the Griffith Park Observatory
and even at the Howard Johnson's
at Hollywood and Vine
they talk about
him.

The Strangler is 5 days away
from Christmas
and he now shops at Zody's
like the rest of us but
with 2 stolen credit
cards.

according to the police
he dresses simply
has brown eyes
walks with a limp
lives with his mother
and has one gold
tooth
in front.

otherwise
he looks no different than anyone
else
except for one thing:
he may be wearing worn
brown sneakers with black
shoelaces.

Happy New
Year.

more mail

I get more and more mail, much of it
gibberish
but now and then a letter will arrive with
some profundity, humor and lucidity.

I am a loner but not a snob.
a good letter deserves a good answer.

and so, a correspondence begins
and, without fail, this is what happens.

the second letter I receive from my
correspondent
seems to have a little less profundity than the
first.

I answer anyhow.

the third letter falls off further.

I try once again.

the fourth letter is actually
idiotic.

I don't respond.

another letter arrives,
almost indecipherable.

I can't reply to this.

then more letters arrive filled with
anger, threats, vindictiveness.

one fellow, getting no response,
sent me a page smeared with
shit.

well, I'm rid of him,
I thought.

not so, another letter soon
arrived as if nothing had
occurred.

what I am getting at here
is the similarity
of all these letter
writers.

a few great beginnings
evaporating to
nothing.

it's as if they just don't have
the strength to
carry on.

they read me
they write me.
and then,
after a while, they hate
me.

and they are all
men.

the women write also
but I don't answer
them.

I know that means
trouble too.

worse trouble.

believe me.

look here!

all my life
while walking around
here and there
I've heard voices—
usually it's two people
approaching me:
"Jesus Christ, *look* at that guy!"
or:
"my god, did you see *that?*"

it happens at supermarkets
at racetracks
in parking lots
in department stores
or when I'm just walking
down the street:
"hey, did you *see* that guy?"

there is evidently another
way a person should look.

I've had them curse me
as I pass:
"that son of a bitch!
did you *see* that fucking bastard?"

I walk on.

there's not much else I
can do.

we can't

we can't win
it
we know we can't win
it
do right and win
it
do wrong and win
it

somebody else is going to win
it

it will happen

but to accept it is
impossible

like a cat I once saw killed and
skinned before my
eyes

and the human
faces
watching.

terrorists

coming up from the street
on the path between
my apartment building and the
building next door
there were explosions
the crash and popping of empty
wine bottles
coming from above
glass skewered and blasting off
in all directions.
I unlocked my door and went inside
it was a good warm afternoon
in late May
the flowers were giving it their best
everywhere.
I took all my clothes off and
stretched out on the
bed.
then I heard voices outside
voices of other people who
lived in my building:
"there are a couple of Puerto Ricans up
there! they live on the roof
next door!"
"they drink and throw their
bottles down!"
"yes, I *know.* I've called the
cops but the cops don't do
nothin'!"
"yeah, they're too busy writing tickets!"
"there's a woman up there on the roof, she's
wearing red leotards!"
"he's wearing a bandanna on his head
and he's always screaming
and throwing things down, bottles,
trash, everything!"
"we'll get up a petition! we'll have
that building *condemned!*"
"yes, a petition! I used to live in

that building! *horrible* things go on
in there!"
"we'll get a petition!"

the next day the manager of my apartment
finds me outside parking my
Volks.
as I get out she
shoves a clipboard at me.
she has 26 signatures already.
"Han ..." she starts to
say.
"no," I say.
"Han ..." she starts to say
again.

in that building live the poor,
the poor Blacks and Mexicans and a
few crazy Orientals.
it's a last chance for them
the last low-rent building
between them and the street.

"Hank," she says, "why
not?"

"because," I tell her, "some day
somebody will get up a petition to get
rid of *me*."

she laughs
not understanding at
all.

I walk on down the path
unlock my door
go inside:
just another crazy white
loser.

big time

I got tired of going to the bars
and then I even got tired of
driving to the liquor store,
I began ordering over the
telephone.
they knew me.
some had read my books.
I could hear them talking
in the background
over the telephone.
they were arguing about
who was going to
deliver the order.
they all wanted to deliver,
they wanted to see the
freak show:
me at the door,
hair hanging in my face,
my beer gut in undershirt,
my red eyes,
my unshaven face,
the bottles on the floor,
the women.
they wanted to see
this.
they thought I was really
living.
I just had this thirst,
that's all.
and the women were
there for the free
drinks.

I always had trouble
getting rid of the
delivery guys.
I'd pay the bill, tip them
and they'd just stand there
in the doorway

looking in.

"you can go now,"
I'd say.

"huh?"

"it's time for you to
vanish."

he'd be staring in
at the women
who weren't really
that much to
look at.

"huh?"

"you're standing in
the doorway.
now move it or I'll
move it for
you!"

he'd step back and
I'd close the
door,
carry the package
back into the
kitchen,
pull out the
bottles and the
cigars
there under the
cheap glaring light.

"hey, for Christ's sake,
bring me a drink!"
I'd hear a voice from
the other room.

"shit, yeah!" I'd hear
another voice.

"keep your pants on,"
I'd say.

"I'm not wearing
any."

"that figures."

in those days everybody
wanted to be
like me.
and these days
they do
too.

it figures.

here we go again

I walked out to my car
and there was a note under my
windshield wiper:
"hey, old man,
give me a call sometime.
you know
I'm listed in the phone
book."
and she signed it:
"light brown eyes."
I knew who it was,
the large writing was instantly
recognizable without the
signature.
she'd had me on the cross for a
year.
she'd followed the one who'd had me
on the cross for five years.
I tore the note up.
then the latest one came walking up
to the car.
"ready to go, Popsie?" she asked.
"ready to go," I said.
we got in and drove off.
we needed lemons, bread, fish,
vegetables, olive oil, wine and
toilet paper.
and cat food and maybe onions
too.

Manx

have we gone wrong again?
we laugh less and less,
become more sadly sane.
all we want is
the absence of others.
even favorite classical music
has been heard too often and
all the good books have been
read...

there is a sliding
glass door
and there outside
a white Manx sits
with one crossed eye
his tongue sticks out the
corner of his mouth.
I lean over
and pull the door open
and he comes running in
front legs working
in one direction,
rear legs
in the other.

he circles the
room in a scurvy angle
to where I sit
claws up my legs
my chest
places front legs
like arms
on my shoulders
sticks his snout
against my nose
and looks at me as
best he can.
also befuddled,
I look back.

a better night now,
old boy,
a better time,
a better way now
stuck together
like this
here.

I am able
to smile again
as suddenly
the Manx
leaps away
scattering across the
rug sideways
chasing something now
that none of us
can see.

the best men are strongest alone

most of the time while a man is trying to
type
some woman is running in and out
she wants this
she wants that.

most of the time while a man is typing
there are simultaneous arguments with some woman.

it's not easy to argue with some woman and type
at the same time.
sometimes I think some women are jealous of
the typewriter.

the typewriter earns them restaurant meals,
a decent car, clothes, shoes.
but they are jealous of the typewriter.
"when you go upstairs to type, I am all
alone," they say.

when I go upstairs to type I am alone
too.
there are times when there wasn't any
upstairs.
there were times when it was one room
with the toilet down the
hall.
there were times when there wasn't a
room or a typer, just a park
bench.

"that typewriter is your crutch,"
they say wisely.

I'm too old to go back to the factory,
the factory would not want me
now.

thankfully

this machine has been as faithful to me
as any woman I have ever known.

and tonight is a special night.
I am alone again
just like when I started.

my fingers rattle the keys.
the war has never ended.
I like this fight.

and it dawns on me now that
there is nothing so beautiful and
pure and as perfect as the well
written line.

another love poem

your toenails are so long, she said,
my god.

and I said,
I never cut my own toenails,
some woman always does it for
me.

she got the clippers and began.

I was in San Francisco
stretched out on the floor.
she was a professional dancer,
we had made love, gone to Fisherman's
Wharf, come back and had some
herb tea, were resting before
making love
again.

she had a roomful of classical records
and books,
even mine.

such toenails, she said, my god.
but hold still, I won't
hurt you.

there, she said, when she was finished
clipping, now you can get another bitch
to cut you next
time.

then she took some oil and began massaging
my toes and feet.

you'll have to rub my neck in
return, she said.

I rubbed her neck to Mozart

and soon we were making love
again.

now I'm back in Los Angeles
sitting in my kitchen
barefooted,
and images of her
keep entering my
mind.

Nina,
I hope the next bitch who cuts my toenails
is you.

the Spanish gate

after the reading we went to her home, a large place
with a beautiful iron gate imported from Spain
and in the house were her lovely daughters who
smiled at me with their lips and their eyes and
their bodies but then
they left
and I sat with the lady in her kitchen and
she showed me her novel published in Europe
many years before. I looked at the cover and flipped through
the pages but I was uninterested in her book:
I had my fee from the reading and a young
girl in a nice house in L.A. was waiting for me.

but
this lady was cultured or
at least seemed to be and
she spoke with a European accent and
I enjoyed sitting and watching her smoke her
long cigarettes.

she told me that I could have my own bedroom that
night and I told her that was fine and
we talked and later that night she showed me
my bedroom and she went off and I climbed under the covers
for a while
then
I got up
found her bedroom and got into bed with her and we did
that ordinary and everynight thing and then
we slept and the next morning
I walked out through her imported Spanish gate and took a
cab to the airport and flew back to my young girl in L.A.
with her own nice
house.

a couple of weeks later we got a package in the mail from
the lady. she had sent her novel that
had been published in Europe by an important publisher
many years before and

she signed it "love" and requested in an enclosed letter
if I would ask my editor now to re-publish her book here in
America.

I read it
and liked it well enough and
mailed it on to my editor.

that was eleven years ago, and my editor hasn't
re-published that book yet
but here's a poem about it.

not much of a poem, you see, and maybe it should not
have been written at all
except
that I really miss
that
beautiful
imported
Spanish
gate.

no dice

reading poetry in this poetry magazine
I feel as if I have been lightly slapped by
a dead fish.
I rise from the bed and move uneasily about
the room
looking for myself.
I am standing over by the closet, grinning.
I walk over, get into myself,
walk down the stairway.
my wife takes note of me, is not
surprised.
I stand before the glass doors which
lead to the yard.
as always, I have this gentle urge to
throw myself through
them.
instead, I go sit on the couch.
my gut bugs out.
my wife is in a peaceful mood.
then the god-damned phone
rings.
our answering machine tells
the caller:
"THERE IS NOBODY HERE,
BELIEVE US."
the caller hangs up without leaving
a message.
we are grateful.
the night comes through the glass
doors.
I get up and let one of the cats
out.
he has blue eyes and wears a
mask.
I stand there looking at my
wife.
"I tried to read some poetry
tonight," I say.
she looks at me.
"I know," she
answers.

stark dead

pretentious pap smeared on sanctified
walls
again and again
until almost everybody believes it is
viable.

affectations of the centuries accepted
as Art.

beware the textbooks, beware the libraries,
beware the galleries,
beware the father and the teacher.
beware the mother.

we are born into a civilization which is stunned
by overwhelming mediocrity.

what is placed before us is artifice, an
illusion, a lie.

the womb has spilled us into a sewer.

new gods are needed.

new doors must be opened.

we have waited so long for so little.

we must rip the enclosures open.

this dark stinks of us,

here.

hello

sometimes even writing doesn't help
and you are there alone with whatever is
killing you
and the senselessness of
the walls penetrate
you
and over in the corner the bottle
sits—
your last friend, your last lover,
your other keyboard.

hello, there.

lunch

I parked in back
and went in to eat.
a new restaurant
a small place
a very small guy
almost a midget
behind the counter.
that's nice, I thought,
a little guy like that,
he's making it, got his
own place but he's very
nervous, why is he so
nervous?
I gave him my order and
told him, "get it started,
I'll be back, I'm going
across the street for a
newspaper."
"o.k.," he said.
there was a Mexican girl
in there mopping the floor.

when I got back the
girl was still mopping and
the guy hadn't started my
order.
he was screaming at the
girl: "hurry up and
finish mopping! the people
are gonna be arriving
soon and you're gonna
have to help me
with the orders!"

"I'm here now," I said,
"you got my order ready?"

"just a minute," he said.
he ran into the crapper

and leaving the door
half open he
flipped the seat down
yanking his pants and
his shorts down
in one motion
as he did so.

"put the god-damned
coffee on!" he screamed
at the girl
as he sat there.

then he was silent
head down
working on
this new problem.
I watched him
finish
making sure he
washed his
hands.

he did
then ran out
and got started on
my order.
the girl was still
mopping.

I sat down
at a small table and
read the headlines:
the Russians were
on the Polish
border again.

I checked the race
results and the
entries.

"o.k.," the little
guy screamed at
me, "it's ready!"

I went over
picked up my order
paid
went back to the
table
began eating
reading:
city councilman accused of
having sex with three minors
giving them drugs
the girls were 14, 15 and
16.
the city councilman
denied the charges.

"finish the mopping!" the guy
screamed at the girl. "have you
made the coffee yet?"

the girl came mopping by my table,
the floor looking very good.
she must have been about 20.
"help me," she said.
she had a thick accent.
"what?" I asked.
"help me!" she repeated
with more emphasis.
her eyes were dark brown and
I could see the panic in
them.

"oh yeah," I smiled back.

she paused
then continued her work.

"come here!" the little guy

screamed at her.

she put her mop in the bucket
and went around behind the counter.

"you don't know nothing!" the little
guy screamed at her. "listen to me and
maybe you'll learn something!"

I finished eating
and walked out
to the back.

as I unlocked
my car
I could see through
the screen door in the
back of the café.
I could hear his
voice
but I couldn't
decipher the
words
all I could see
were his arms
waving
as he screamed

she was in a
short red dress and
flat white shoes
as she stood
before him
and listened.

I got
into the car
started it and
backed out of the
parking lot
into the

alley
cut right
down the alley
took
a left
up the next
street
then
a right
and then
I was at
the freeway
and
on my way.

four young gang-bangers

you know how women can get.
they can *goad* you.
I was fighting with my girlfriend
and I was fighting mad.
we were arguing over the phone
and I said *that's it!*
and she said *that's it!*
and we hung up.

I went to the racetrack that
night and played all the
longshots
and I bet heavily because I didn't care
and I kept winning damn near every race
but that only made me angry
because there was nobody around to see
how good I was even when
I wasn't trying and that in particular
only made me even more unhappy.

then the races were over and I had
all that cash but it didn't matter to me
as I drove up 8th Avenue
and stopped at a traffic signal.
it was a bad part of town
and the car behind me
began to push up against my rear bumper.

I looked back and there were four
young gang-bangers in the car behind me.

I pulled away from the signal
then pulled over to the curb and waited
let them go by me
then I started up and got behind them
and began to tailgate them.
at every stop sign I rammed their
rear bumper.

they started to speed up,
taking the corners and going down side streets.
I followed, making sharp turns,
skidding, I kept as close as I could to the rear
of their car.

then their car pulled up
and they just sat and waited
near a dark playground.
I pulled up behind them
opened my door
leaped out and
ran over to them.

their car jumped off
into the night.
I ran back, leaped into
my car, took off after them,
took a right where they
had turned but

they were gone...

I never told my girlfriend about it
after we got back together
but I did tell her
that I had won 12 or
13 hundred dollars.

"it was a lucky night for
you," she said.

"you're certainly right,"
I replied.

I don't care

I can't do it anymore, any of it, I'm turning in my
badge at last, it's what THEY'VE BEEN
WAITING FOR:
now they can dance in the street
and their envy can turn gentle:
"yeah, I gotta admit Chinaski *could* write a
little bit in the old days..."

it's been over a week and I haven't written a
decent line, and writing was never difficult
for me before.

I walk across the room, catch a look at
myself in the mirror:
how long did you think
you'd be able to play with words?
everything ends eventually so
stop your whining.

damn, I never had a problem with writing before.

62. what will I do?
go sit in the park with the other old farts?

who would ever have thought you'd last this long
anyway?

it's the first hot night of summer, one
bottle of wine is now gone as the radio plays
gloomy chamber music.

I will say one thing, however, it's nice here now
even with everything else gone wrong, not to be
arguing with my woman tonight.
she's gone off somewhere
and this
poem which never really got started
is now done and
the second bottle of wine is waiting

for me.

now, there's an art I can still
handle.

Royal Standard

bad nights can't be cured by bad poems, you
have to wait, look at a doorknob, read the newspaper
over again

you are not the only one having a bad night, it's a
world full of bad nights

and it's enough sometimes just to have a typewriter
and to
smoke a cigarette
and just look at the machine

and wonder about all the good luck you've had
with that machine and
the other machines

yet
one is spoiled
one wants
more and more

and now my fingers
tap the keys
and tell you and
it

about all that.

Mother and Princess Tina

we knew it was a tourist trap, of course, but sometimes you
     go in
anyway.
PRINCESS TINA was performing
on the far side of the harbor,
in a floating restaurant/bar,
valet parking available.
a dinner table for four would be a thirty-minute wait but
meanwhile there was the bar with orchestra and dancing and
(of course) PRINCESS TINA.
we got our drinks and it was terrible in there:
the patrons, the singing, the drinks.

I kept looking at the 50 or 60 faces
in some wild search for something real.
then I found two big heads on two big bodies:
he stretching his legs leisurely under the table
and she just sitting there with her big beer gut hanging out.
all the other passengers were less than nothing

"look," I told the others at our table,
"over there. the only two real people in here."
they looked. the music ended.
then the m.c. at the mike asked,
"now, who would like to hear their favorite
song?"

my man with the big head stood up and looked
around and said,
"well, since this is Mother's Day I think we ought to
have a song for *Mother!*
I don't think any of us loved our Mother
enough!"

so the orchestra launched into a Mother's Day song
and it was danceable and the two big heads
got up and danced
their bodies far apart and kicking their heels
high the way ranch people dance in Arizona and

260

New Mexico and Utah and Wyoming.

as it ended our dinner table was ready and we went on
in and the *maître d'* told us, sorry, but the air-conditioning
has broken down. my chair had one short
leg and when the food finally arrived it wasn't
very much either.

late night

the man on the radio speaks of the
last hour of Sodom.
earlier he had spoken of the
last Seven Words of Christ.

my cat walks in.
I look at him.
he's all fur, eyes, tail, legs,
claws, whiskers.

I change the radio station.
there is a flute solo.
long string-like loops of
melody.

I find a federal reserve note on
the desk.
there are two large 5's in the
upper corners,
two smaller 5's in the lower,
also four smaller 8's further
within the bill.
there are also 8 serial numbers
duplicated twice.

how many numbers on the
Lincoln side of a 5 dollar bill?
24.
you can win a bet this
way.

I change the radio station
again.
a lady sings,
"*Don't get me wrong,
it wasn't easy
getting over you ...*"

the cat walks out and I
get up to go to the bedroom
to
sleep.

night sweats

it was all right at first when I moved here: on the third
day my neighbor to the east saw me
trimming the hedge and offered me his
electric hedge-trimmer.
I thanked him but told him I needed the exercise.
then I leaned down and petted his tiny quivering
dog.
he told me that he was 83 years old
but still went to work every day.
it was his company and they did a million dollars
worth of business every month.
I couldn't match that so I didn't say anything.
then he told me that if I ever needed anything
to let him and/or his wife know.
I thanked him, then went back to the hedge.

each night I could see his wife watching television.
she looked at the same programs I did.
then one night I felt tense or something and I
ran up and down the stairway screaming at the woman I
live with. (some nights I scream loudly and dramat-
ically, running about naked, for an hour or
two, then I go to bed and fall asleep.)

I did this twice during the second week
of living here.
now I no longer see his wife watching television.
the venetian blinds are drawn closed,
and I no longer see the old man and his tiny
quivering dog,
also I no longer see my neighbor to the west
(although on the 4th day I gave him some tangerines
from my tangerine tree).

everybody has vanished.

come to think of it
even my woman isn't here tonight.

locks

I moved into a new place and decided to change the locks.
I phoned the nearest locksmith and he told me
I needn't change the locks, he could make new keys.

"all you have to do," he said, "is take
the locks out and bring them down here.
just remove the 3 little screws
and pull the locks out."

the side door wasn't difficult.
I pulled the lock out and put it carefully into
a cardboard box.
then
I went to the front door and it seemed simple
only the front door handle came off and
I thought,
I wonder if he needs the handle too?
I put everything into the cardboard box and got into
the car and drove down to the locksmith.

"are you the guy who phoned?" he asked me.
I told him that I was and then he asked,
"do you have the key?"
I gave him the key and he took it and the locks and the handle
and disappeared into his shop.

I stood out in the alley behind the place and waited.
the only view was the back of a Chevron gas station.
I looked at it for quite a while then
I walked over to my car and looked at it for a while
and then
I lit a cigarette and walked back.
the man had the keys ready.
"$10," he said.
I asked him if he might tell me a little bit about re-
installing locks.
"sure," he said, "now this part fits here. it
doesn't matter which part you stick in here,
either end will do."

I asked him if either end would do then why did one end
have a nodule on it while the other end was flat?
"that's a good question," he said, "now this
part, these two prongs slip in here, you hold
it together against the front of the lock and
tighten the 3 screws. also, when you do this
make sure the lock is in the locked position."

I drove the locks back to my place and
I tried the side door first and everything seemed to
fit all right, it locked and unlocked, although
there was space around the lock and the door itself
and it wouldn't slide in flush.

then
I tried the front door
I put the handle back on
then
I slipped the parts together.
there was some trouble pushing the screws in against
the wood and getting them started but then it was done but
it wasn't right: the latch was locked against
the handle and it wouldn't lift up.

I phoned my girlfriend and told her that
I just couldn't install door locks.
"it's easy," she said, "I've changed dozens myself,
there's nothing to it."
I told her that it wasn't easy because even when they told
you some things they left other things out.
"just forget the locks," she said, "I'll fix them
when I get there."
the problem was that she wasn't coming until the next day.

I uncorked some wine and sat down at the typewriter and
turned on the radio and smoked cigars and typed.
I drank the wine and smoked and typed until somewhere
between one and two a.m. then
I walked over to the bed, fell on it and slept.
I awakened 30 minutes later, took off my clothes and slid
under the blankets.

about 4:30 a.m.
I awakened and thought about the front door and
I got up and went downstairs naked.
I got the screwdriver and went to work but the lock parts
became scrambled.
I tried to put the lock back in, checking for the slot
for the latch tongue and then
I found that
I had lost one of the 3 screws necessary to fasten the lock
back together again.
I turned on all the lights but it was dark down on the
floor so
I turned on the front porch light but I still couldn't find
the screw so
I walked naked to the garage and looked in the glove
        compartment of
the car and got the flashlight out and came back up on the
porch, got down on my knees and flicked it on and it died
after about ten seconds.
I gathered all the lock parts together and put them in a little
pile, then
I closed the door and turned out all the lights.
there was now a large hole in the door where
the moonlight came through.
I found three chairs and stacked them up against the closed door
and then
I went upstairs and got back into bed.

in the morning
I phoned the locksmith and told him that
I couldn't manage it and wasn't there somebody he could
send up? and I told him about the 3 screws. that
I had lost one of them.

"you were the guy in the white t-
shirt, weren't you?" he asked.
"yes," I said.
"we'll have a man up there in a
couple of hours."

I waited until 12 p.m. and then

I phoned again and
I told him that
I was the guy in the white t-shirt and that
I had phoned earlier and that
I had an important business appointment that afternoon
(it was one of the last days of the Oak Tree meet,
first post, 12:30 p.m.)
and that I *could* cancel my appointment but
I'd certainly prefer not to.

"I have another man coming in at 12:15," he said.
"we'll have him up there in a couple of
minutes."

the man arrived at 1:05 and
I told him there were supposed to be 3 screws and that
I had lost one of them.

"nice place you got here," he told me.
he picked up the lock and began fitting it together
and he said,
"no, you haven't lost a screw, here it is stuck
in the back of the lock."

I stood there and watched him slip the lock into the
hole in the door.
then he pulled the lock out of the door.
"you know," he said, "this is a very complicated
lock, it's expensive and more difficult to fit
together."

then he jiggled the lock parts and slipped them
back into the door.
then he pulled the parts out again.

"I don't understand it," he said
looking at the doorknob.
"the doorknob's frozen so I'll have to fix
the doorknob first."

he sat down on the steps and twisted at the door

knob and
I walked to a table in the other room and sat where
I could see him.
there was a newspaper there
I had already read and
I began to read it again.

5 or ten minutes went by and
I said,
"look, let's just replace everything ... new knob,
new lock and I'll pay for everything."

"wait," he said, "give me a chance."

I read the newspaper some more,
I read through the whole front section.
then the repairman stood up:
"I'll be back, I'm going to have to lubricate
this thing ..."

he was gone for about twenty minutes and when he
came back the doorknob was no longer frozen and he
fit the lock parts back in and bolted them home.
then he stuck the key in and it worked.

"it works but there's still something wrong here that
I don't understand."

"it's strange," I said, "I had very little trouble
putting the lock in the side door."

"you mean," he asked, "that there are *two* locks?"

"yes, didn't someone tell you?"

"no. then that's the trouble: let me see the other
lock."

I showed him the other lock.
"it's falling out," I said, "but it works."

he told me, "you mixed the parts of the two locks.
they are different locks."

then he took out both locks
rearranged the parts the way they should be
put the locks back in and both of them
worked just fine.

"that'll be fifteen dollars," he said.

I thought that was very reasonable and handed him a
twenty.

"damn it," he said, "I don't have any change.
don't you have any change?"

"no, all I have are twenties."

"you'll need a receipt?"

"yes, so I can take it off my income tax."

he offered to drive me down to the corner market and
I'd get change
and we got into his truck and drove down to the
market and
I went in and got two bottles of wine and change for one of
my twenties.
I came out and handed him his $15 and told him to forget the
receipt.
I usually lost them anyhow long before tax time.

"I'll give you a ride back,"
he said.

so we drove back up the hill and
I missed the running board getting out
but managed not to fall as he
drove off.

I walked up the drive with my two bottles of wine

stuck the key into the door and it opened.
I sat down, corkscrewed the bottle open and poured
a drink, then
I telephoned my girlfriend.

"it's too late for the races but I got the locks
fixed."

"I could have done it,"
she said. "it's so simple.
I could have saved you money!"

"I know," I said, "but you weren't here."

40 minutes later
I was at the racetrack as they were coming out
for the 5th race.

token drunk

I was standing on the deck near the rail
when a young man walked up to me
and asked, "are you the token drunk?"
the boat was full of media people, models,
photographers, script writers, etc.
there had just been a wedding and I had made
myself two turkey sandwiches and was working
on the champagne.
the man started talking about movies
as I stood there thinking, I've missed a
day at the racetrack.
things were always getting in the way of the
racetrack: weddings, trips to Europe, interviews
and illness.

my girlfriend was talking to a fat German in dark glasses.
it wasn't going to be a very good party.
"pardon me," I said to my fellow, "but I've got to
get some more turkey."

when I came back I had this nice little girl with me;
she was such a nice girl that I didn't even
think about sex.
she worked for the bride and I knew the bride and
we talked about her job working for the bride.
then I told the girl, "if I don't make trouble at
these parties then there just isn't any trouble. I
don't see why I always have to be the one who makes
the trouble."
"I've heard that you *do* cause trouble," she said.
"really?" I asked, putting my hand on
her ass.
"really," she said.
then I squeezed her ass while
we kept talking and soon we all went into the cabin, the
girl, my girlfriend, the German with the dark glasses and
myself.
the drinks were inside and the drinks were running
low.

I was getting worried when the groom walked in and
told us, "we are going to the Beverly Hills Hotel ..."

when I awakened I was in a strange bed but my girlfriend
was with me so it was all right.

"well," she said, "you pulled your old knife trick
again, you pulled your knife on the *maître d'* and
the waiters in the Polo Lounge and now you'll never
be able to go to the Beverly Hills Hotel again."

"I shouldn't carry that thing," I said, "I always
forget."

"they were going to call the police but we talked them
out of it, then we drove over here and you smashed the
front of your car because you couldn't find reverse
gear, you rammed the phone pole and you wanted to
smash the car next to you because you didn't like the
way it was parked but you couldn't find reverse gear so
you gave up."

I got up and began to dress.
"let's get out of here. where are we?"

"we're at the Hansens'."

Hansen was a big-time camera man.

I walked out. Hansen was there, Mrs. Hansen was in Paris;
there was also an actor there reading the funny papers and
a director staring out at the ocean.

"we're getting ready," I told them, "we'll be going soon."

somebody coughed.
my girlfriend came out and we walked to the car.
there was broken glass on the ground.
I got into reverse without trouble
but scraped the side of the car against a cement
abutment.

272

then I drove off the wrong way down a one-way street.
I noticed that right away and
took a left at the next corner.
it was just another Sunday morning in
Marina del Rey.

Butch Van Gogh

just before leaving East Hollywood my cat got
into a fight that left
him with a cauliflower ear.
now that we're settled in San Pedro
I took him to a vet yesterday.
they had an EMERGENCY room
they had animal dentistry
shock therapy
electrocardiogram
preanesthetics
operating room
psychiatric clinic with
psychological evaluation and
behavior modification
a dermatology clinic
intensive care unit
private nurses and
24-hour medical observation
along with the usual
pills and
ointments.

the estimate
came to $182.50
and there would be additional charges for
follow-up treatment and medication.

"Jesus," I told the vet, "this is a ten-year-old de-
balled alley cat. I can get a dozen of these for
nothing."

the vet just made little circles on a piece of paper
with his pencil.

"all right," I said, "go ahead."

"Butch Chinaski," the vet wrote down the patient's
name.

when I went back to get him 3 hours later
they had most of his skull wrapped and
he had a little wet hole drilled in the side
of his head. he came out of room 6
carried by a nurse in a tight white skirt.

"what'd you do?" I asked, "give him a
lobotomy?"

we're back home now. he just sits on top of
the stove and stares at me. he's unhappy. he's
Butch Van Gogh Chinaski.

like a friend of mine once told me:
"man, everything you touch turns to shit!"

he's right.

I don't want Cleopatra

I am always exposing myself.
I go out on the front porch in my shorts
bend over to pick up the paper and
my parts fall out.

I sunbathe nude in the backyard
and sometimes stand up.
"you fool," my girlfriend says,
"Mrs. Catherty can see you over the
wall!"
"where is she?" I ask.
"she's standing right there watering her
rose bushes!"
"oh ..."
"get *down!*"

to me, nudity is a joke.
I don't think nude people are attractive
at all.
I like my women fully clothed.
I like to imagine what might be under
there.
it might not be what you'd expect.

imagine stripping a woman down
and she has a body like a little submarine
with a periscope, propellers, a few torpedoes.

she would be the one for me!
I'd marry her right off and
be faithful to the end.

the strange workings of the dark life

he lived in Canada and in a famous
encounter he outboxed
Hemingway
but he couldn't write as well as
Hemingway.

I remember years ago,
and I speak of the racetrack
now,
one of the lesser jocks beat up
one of the leading jocks.
this got him some attention
for a while
but the leading jock kept
winning
as usual
and the one who kicked his
ass
could still barely get a horse to
the wire.

of course, what made
Hemingway's defeat more
awful
was his manly stance, his
self-proclaimed
prowess, his
masculinity.

still, there isn't a man
alive,
good as he might be with
his fists,
who at a given moment,
even in the prime of his life,
can't be taken out
by somebody
somewhere.

me, I'm lucky:
I never claimed to be
good at fighting,
only that I had been
in any number of
fights
and that I remember
my few
victories
with delight and
wonder.

my main claim to fame
was that I could take
a great punch,
many great punches
(and unfortunately
I did)
which I think
(with my poor
brain pounded
down to
nothing)
somehow led to
my learning how
to get the word
down
using a simple
line and an
uncluttered
style
(never taught in the
universities)
thank the devil
and thank the bluebird
in the mouth of the cat
with the tender whiskers
and the padded feet of
death.

open all night

on a train somewhere in Europe, down to the last drink, the
evening and sleeplessness at hand, tired of watching small villages
go by lived in by people sensible enough to stay in their own
beds (a good place to endure life and wait for no more of
it).

she's asleep on your shoulder as you try to wish the
half glass of wine in your hand into a full glass just
as you also wish you were anywhere but here.
travel broadens, they say, but it's not true, it lessens,
it confuses, it diminishes, it floods down through the top
of the skull and leaks out of your eyes. there's this senseless
necessity to come to terms with something new you don't quite
understand.

you drink the half glass, waiting for the tongue to send
mercy to the mind; it doesn't happen.
you set the glass, the empty glass, upon the window
sill, looking out at the warm and colorful village roofs
as just then the drunken troops of some army arrive:
young boys staggering toward manhood bang along the vesti-
bule, singing badly, almost frightened, still too close
to mother's arms but *loud*, you know, maybe some of them
now brave with drink.
they are trained to obey, kill and be killed.
some of them lurch against the compartment door as they
move past
yearning and dreaming of women and victory.

I get up, stand at the compartment door. they look in,
leer in, some slam their fist against the glass; there's
energy there as they yell and sing, there's energy there
that needs to be used.
I wave, wink, or remain impassive before each passing
face, depending upon their mood or mine, depending upon
what bluff or what force or what determination or
resistance or embrace is necessary.
they keep coming by: there must be half a fucking army.

hey, boys, I was born here just like you. see me?
I'm German. notice the shape of the skull; bulldog jaw; the
nasty fearful eyes. I was born in Andernach on the Rhine.
got an uncle there 93 years old.

I am frightened and I am not frightened; I am ready for
them and it feels good to be ready, whatever is coming I'm
going to get somebody's balls, somebody is going to lose
a retina or an ear at least before they halve my skull
and dip pretzels into my nervous brain...

then they're gone, the last mother's son, white faces
like flattened aspirin tablets and maybe now I'll be able
to listen to Sibelius' Fifth soon again.

I take off my shoes and slide onto the long narrow
seat we use for a bed.
she has stretched out comfortably while I was confront-
ing that battalion and I lay down beside her,
put my arm around her waist to keep me from rolling onto
the floor as we sleep, as she sleeps, as I attempt to
sleep.

she is a good girl. in the morning as the light comes
through the thick, dirty train window, lighting the
stained drinking glass, she'll get
up, go to the bathroom in our little compartment,
then come and find me looking gloomy dull dumb
defeated, sleepy and sleepless, smiling grimly.
she'll get out the map and tell me of the castles
and vineyards to come, of vivid landscapes and
miracles, and I'll be pleased by her excitement but
the world and its history and its ways will confuse me
as always and I'll want to leave that train and
leave this place and I'll want badly to go home, wherever
that is.

but now the troops are gone and the last drink is gone
and the night is gone
and I wait
dreamless and unsatisfied
like almost all the other people.

come back

in Mannheim it was always the same: start
out with a couple of steam beers at a table off the
avenue, 10 a.m., sitting with a couple of German
friends, nothing else to do; a couple of steam beers
calls for a couple more steam beers.

something was needed to cure the night before.
the night had been bad, according to my girlfriend.
me singing and screaming, acting up in the bathroom, a
great echo chamber: "EVERYTHING DIES! BLACKBIRDS
DIE! BYE BYE, BLACKBIRD! MAKE MY BED AND LIGHT
   THE
LIGHT ...!"

the night manager rang us three times.

now, more steam beer. now, some white wine. got to
cure the night. then go to bed early.

never anything to eat. by the time you get up the hotel
kitchen is closed. in Germany everything keeps closing
down. the cafés close down between 2 and 5 p.m.
by 5 you're too drunk to eat. Germany is a
bigger drunk than America. even the abstainers
drink wine because you can't drink the water. almost
everybody in Germany is rich; the poor die of thirst.

tougher bars in Germany than in East L.A., run through
with gangs of neo-Nazis with their killer dogs.
if you want to go to the crapper you better smile, wave,
nod, wink at them, or else.

nothing to do but drink and wait for the sun to go down
and for the sun to come up.

or you find yourself in some little café up in the hills
near the vineyards, sometime after one a.m. or two
a.m. or three a.m. where you eat snails, sausages
and asparagus for the price of a week's income.

the people with you seem pleased; but for you
it's not all that interesting or pleasant. because finally
you'll just shit it all out.

one thing you learn, that you have to learn: you must
stop thinking too much: all the boat rides down the Rhine full
of loud Americans, camera brains loaded with exposed film; all
those toy train rides to nowhere—looking out the window
at everything so clean and neat; colorful painted rooftops
passing by and under each roof probably a personal hell for
each one of them inside.

you stop thinking because thinking simply isn't useful
over there.
you cling to a single thought: that you will *leave,*
finally, after you've done your bit for the publishers and
the editors and the girlfriend.

and finally you *do* leave, too many suitcases about, most of
them hers, standing in the lobby at the desk, paying up with
thousands and thousands of DM's, feeling raped and plundered
by the Hun; the night clerk now sleeping it off; the day clerk,
genial, bowing, classy and cultured—"I think he owns the place,"
my girl whispers, "and I think he likes us."

that's good, that's good, the maid rushing up, getting another
tip on top of what we've left in the room. "oh, give her *more* than
that, she was so *sweet* with the orange juice!" so, I give her
more.

we are all hugging, hugging each other, we move toward
the exit, dragging overloaded suitcases, hugging, smiling,
waving. I am ashamed.

and then to the airport. German police, stiff, looking
frightened but ready, standing with fingers on rifle triggers.
they are in a panic of alertness. strange things are occurring
in the world; there is such a thing as terrorism to contend
with now.

waving goodbye, waving goodbye to German friends, and

then we are up and flying, quickly the earth drops away.

I ask the stewardess how long before the first drink and the
whore ignores me, moving away through the bad dream, showing
     me
her buttocks, her aft parts. she's probably a nice girl at home,
pet dog, good to her mother, goes down on her boyfriend but
flying through space, she's the enemy.

my girl is on my shoulder, she's crying, "oh, I hate to leave!
it was so nice! so nice!"

the worst thing for me is not having somebody to talk
to when something obvious must be said; but then
if I had that maybe something else would be missing, and
I catch the stewardess the next time by and she says, "yes, yes,
I will bring you a drink in a moment!"

winging toward terrible America,
my world returning to normal.

4

lazy in San Pedro

my father wanted me to be
a mechanical draftsman but

I decided to be a writer.
it's easy.
I just sit and pick at the ancient scabs and blackheads
of my life
until something comes along.
when the phone rings I pick it up and then gently put it down.
it's so easy.
downstairs my girlfriend reads about Scott and Zelda.
"we're Scott and Zelda," I tell her.
then she gets mad.

I get terrible letters in the mail.
people want to come by and see me.
they send me letters about their lives and enclose poems.
my advice to all young writers is to stop writing the way I do.
I mean, it won't help.
the editors are just going to say,
"Jesus, this guy writes just like Chinaski.
send it back!"

the best thing about writing is that it never
lets you down.
it might let other people down but not you.
like you can find your wife fucking your best friend
on the couch at 3 a.m.
and you can run upstairs and type a poem and
get even with both of them.

I really never liked Scott or Zelda for what they wrote.
it was what they thought and how they lived free.
of course they knew Hemingway and Hemingway knew Miró and
Miró knew Picasso and Picasso knew Joyce and Joyce
probably knew D. H. Lawrence and D. H. knew A. Huxley who
     thought
he knew everything
but like I said I admired the way Scott and Zelda lived
free of all the rules
and my father wanted me to be a mechanical draftsman

but it pleases me more to sit here and write
anything I want to while
looking over the balcony into San Pedro harbor
it's easy
all the scabs and blackheads were worth it.

rest period

he lay in his bed and he was a great
novelist, poet and short story
writer.
visitors were often told that it was
his "rest period"
and were sent
away.

he was visited by a lady
who was a short story writer and
a novelist.
the lady wrote about her visit
to him
in a short story.
she said that he treated her
unkindly,
seemed ungrateful for her
visit.
that maybe he was
not so great
after all.
in her story
she wrote that
"he was a very bitter
man."

he later died of his TB
and the lady's short story
was published.

he was D. H. Lawrence
and she has
rightfully
been long
forgotten.

vultures seldom are blessed with
immortality.

swivel chair

I broke two chairs lately
while typing.
when
the last one broke
I came crashing down at
3 a.m.
and never finished
the poem.

now I have purchased a
Lazy Boy swivel chair.
from the alleys of starvation
I have come all the way up
to this.
what a sardonic salute
to my past!

I can spin around.
lean back.

I've got everything
but a call button to push
and a secretary.

this Lazy Boy swivel has
many uses:

now I'm the tail gunner
in a bomber.
I swing up, down,
around...

rat tat tat tat!

I'm shooting enemy planes
out of the sky.

or, now I'm the *boss.*
I call in some slump-

shouldered dolt
who has been working
hungover
all day.

I lean back,
look him over, he's
not much.

"Chinaski," I tell him,
"I gotta toss your ass out of
here. you're
finished! you ain't been
carrying your
weight! this is no
welfare project!"

he just stands there
saying nothing.

I spin my chair
look at my bookkeeper
sitting there with her
dress hiked up to her
ass.

"Mary Lou," I tell her,
"make out this fellow's
check. give him an extra
day. it's worth it just to
get him
out of here!"

"all right, sir," Mary Lou
says to me.

I watch Chinaski pick up
his check and
slink off.

then I

light a cigar.

there's a new guy standing
in front of me.
he wants a job.

I rattle the application
he has filled out and
stare at it.
I puff on my expensive
cigar.
I glance up at
him.

"you don't seem," I
smile, "to be qualified."

"I know I can do the job, sir,"
he says.

I ball up his application,
toss it into the
wastebasket.

"you're wasting my time,
asshole! please do me
a favor and
leave before I have you
thrown out!"

as he leaves
I lean back
puff on my cigar
exhale
look over at
Mary Lou
and smile.

yes, put a man behind
a desk
in a swivel chair

and big things begin to
happen.

it's true
this old desk
was already here
when I moved
in but
now I have my
swivel.

I'm ready.

rat tat tat tat.

I gotta protect my
fucking literary empire.
I like it.

I swivel to my right
and there tacked to my
bulletin board
is a photo
of Céline.

I swivel to my left
and there
hung on the wall is a
two-by-three-foot
color photo
of a World War I
Fokker tri-plane.

I've come a long way from
skid row, baby, and
I've got a long happy way
to go.

rat tat tat tat!

GOTCHA!

AT&T

now, you see,
we have the buildings and
we have the people and
we put the people in the
buildings and we give
some of them good jobs and some
of them not-such-good jobs
and we give
all of them telephones
and we take them
all different ages and all
different sizes and the
telephones ring and
sometimes the people are in and
sometimes the people are out as the
telephones ring some more
long distance and
short distance as
the buildings stand there and
the hardest time for the people
caught in the buildings
are the holidays: 4th of July,
Labor Day, Thanksgiving, Christ-
mas, New Year's as the
telephones ring
and never stop as
the buildings stand there (and
Saturday and Sunday are
hard times too) as
the telephones ring as
the fog comes in
the rain comes down and
sometimes there's snow as
the telephones ring
all those telephones ringing
ringing ringing
with all the people caught
in the buildings.

now you see it's really
hurtful but nobody
will say so and that's
hurtful too as the
telephones ring as the
buildings stand there as
all the people caught in
the buildings sit and
wonder and work and
wait.

loosely loosely

loosely in the universe,
undone
by rubber snakes and the jimjam
man.

grossly floating hither and yon
then
chopped-up
by Felix the Cat
and wrapped in a gunnysack
along with
Baby Ruth.

the jimjam man
and Felix the Cat,
Bingo Louie and his half-
screwy mother
doing the black bottom
sweet water
grey-blue
wet-belly
waltz.

loosely relegated now
to standing in ponchos
dripping stale rain water:
the weight is at the back of the neck
the pelvis burns in diamond glow
and little children weep
narcotic
among the tadpoles.

the jimjam man is back with
ax, weasel and
tweezers. sounds occupy his fingers
like the humming of
elevators. he shuts off the brightly burning
night and inserts a stick of Wrigley's
Spearmint gum. honor slowly

descends.
shuffleboard tables rattle in their
glory.

the palace is under a rock
once walked over by a very blue peacock
under a very orange
sun.

alleluliah! alleluliah! alleluliah!
alleluliah! alleluliah! alleluliah!

fungoes

hit 'em high,
make the fielder go back for
it,
make him run,
looking up into the sun,
burn that belly off
him,
he's lucky to have the
job,
2 million a year for chasing
a little white round ball
or trying to hit
it.
unimpressive fellow, really,
with his dull dirty jokes in
the locker room.

he got that one.
now I'll run his ass from center
to right.
he's only 25 been married and divorced 3
times,
one of those guys who has to always
have a woman,
his tongue hanging out like
a hound dog in
July.

he barely makes the catch.

I wave him on in.

he comes loping in, this
millionaire sheathed in
beer sweat.

"don't want you to have a
heart attack, kid," I tell
him.

"shit," he says, "I could go
another 20 minutes."

"yeah," I tell him, "on a
stretcher."

"fuck you, Pop," he
says,
then walks to the
dugout.

his latest girlfriend and
his tax consultant are
sitting in the stands.
they wave to him.
he nods back.

I take the fungo bat,
crack one over the left
field wall.

then I trot around the
bases thinking, it's a hell of
a spring.
bastards like that really
get on my
nerves.

Schubert

when I was much younger than I am now
I used to be a sucker for Art movies
and I saw many of them when I lived
in Greenwich Village—
the French produced a string of them
with English subtitles—
arms suddenly leaping out of the backs
of sofas; snowballs thrown into the face
of a sensitive schoolboy; and many films
about the lives of the great composers who were
always starving and unhappy and having
troubles with their beautiful ladies.
I suppose that really their ladies
weren't so beautiful and they had no
more troubles with their women than we do with
ours, but it was convenient to think that it was so,
good to imagine that there were
men with troubles, souls and
talents greater than ours, as surely must have been the
case.

I remember sitting there one night when
Schubert's girlfriend left him a
note saying, "I am leaving you for your
own good."

now I didn't like that
because I knew that people usually
leave other people for their *own* good,
which usually means they want to be with somebody
else.
and when Schubert got the note,
he read it and said,
"now I must turn my face to God."

I got up and walked out so I don't know
how that one ended.

I suppose those movies helped me somehow

because at that time I thought I was an artist
even though my short stories
kept coming back from *The New Yorker*
and I too was starving and unhappy while
the whole world was at war
and there were plenty of jobs.

you get a lot of nuts who like to
watch those Art movies.

problems in the checkout line

often in the supermarket checkout line
the cashier will ask me,
"how are you?"
and I'll answer something
like, "not so good, I've got
hemorrhoids, insomnia, vertigo and
the battery in my watch is
dead."

there's never a response, it's as if
they haven't heard, they just keep
ringing up my purchase.

I am not attempting to take out my
frustrations on supermarket
employees
but when they ask me
"how you are?"
I'm usually not doing very well and there's nothing that
makes me feel worse
than to say,
"fine."

I've tried another way.
when they ask
"how are you?"
I say, "it's never been so
good! it's unbelievable! the money's
just rolling in! I don't understand
it!"

but they dislike this reply
more than the
hemorrhoid, insomnia, vertigo
bit.

so I've tried a third way.
when they ask that same question
I say,

"you really don't care."

again there's no reaction, they
just go on
ringing up my purchase
and I understand this lack
of response:
they really *don't* care,
and I think that's good.
we all ought to realize that it's
nothing to be ashamed of
and it makes buying
groceries
the same as
anything else:
what we need is what we want and
what we want
has very little to do
with anything
else.

troubles in the night

son-of-a-bitch, I don't know why
late at night he keeps playing
the *Pathétique*.

he plays it as I sit here naked
as a pink pig
while I type.

I get through the days. now
down at this radio station the host
(I don't know his name)
keeps playing the *Pathétique* late at night
which only reminds me of the
billions of bones buried in the earth
and of
all my x-girlfriends now with other
men.
honeysuckle summer madness.

the day has now passed into night.
night is when I think of going
quietly to bed,
letting the starlight puzzle over
my senseless life;
I don't want any heavy
thoughts
I don't want to be reminded of
the rankness of
life.
it makes me
fitful and inept and
sleepless until the first light of
the next day.

this nameless host at the radio station
this son-of-a-bitch
whatever happened to his waltz
records?

I change stations, and there's some
maniac singing
"she tried to hitch me to her wagon,
she wants to drive me like a mule ..."

I turn the radio off and
when I look down there's a spider
walking across my desk.
he's just walking along
by himself
without a web or
anything.

honeysuckle summer madness ...

I name him Tchaikowsky,
Peter Illich Tchaikowsky (1840–1893)
then I press my hand down and
kill him,
walk to the bedroom thinking,
I will write that son-of-a-bitch
down at the radio station
(knowing all along that I won't)
and tell him how I feel.
I fall on the bed
face-down
my body resting over the
millions and billions of bones
buried in the earth
and all the billions of bones
to follow,
son-of-a-bitch,
including mine.

dead spider, please forgive me, if I had
been anywhere else instead of here
listening to the *Pathétique*
you'd probably have caught a juicy
fly by now.

where to put it

don't blame me if your car breaks down on the freeway.
don't blame me if your wife runs away.
don't blame me if you went to war and discovered that people kill.

don't blame me that you murdered 4 years by voting for the
    wrong man.
don't blame me that sex sometimes fails.

don't blame me if I don't answer the telephone and can't watch
    tv.

don't blame me for your father.
don't blame me for the corner church.
don't blame me for the hydrogen bomb.

blame me if you're reading this.
don't blame me if you don't understand it.

don't blame me that the world crawls with killers.
don't blame me if you're one of them.
blame your father.
blame the corner church.

don't blame me for Christmas or the 4th of July.
blame anybody else you fucking want to but don't blame me.

don't blame me for the homeless.
don't blame me for 162 baseball games every year.
don't blame me for basketball.

don't blame me for not wanting to get in crowded elevators.
don't blame me for not having a hero.
don't blame me for not creating one.

don't blame me for being confused by the laughter of the masses.
don't blame me for laughing alone.

don't blame me for the caging of the tiger.

blame me that my death will not be fearful,

but don't blame yourself.

parodies himself, romanticizes himself.
he's in a small room again,
always in a small room, closing the door,
closing out the
world.
in his 70s he's still trying to over-
come his brutal childhood
and he's never had a real understanding
of women.
his writing is uneven
if powerful
and even at its best there is a feeling
of redundancy,
of nothing new.
he has been imitated by hordes
of writers
who find his simple style
appealing.
he now has a home, a swimming
pool, a spa, a fine car
and a wife who feeds him
vitamins.
he is a recluse
and if you approach him at the
racetrack
there is a chance you will be
ignored or insulted.
his only visitors appear to be
movie stars,
film directors and
interviewers.
upon his death
perhaps a small place will be
made for him
in world literature
where he will sulk in the
shadow of Céline, Hemingway, Jeffers
and Henry Miller.
God rest his alcoholic

agnostic
soul
and now let us go on to
more worthwhile
things.

hummingbird chance

held to this life, neatly, walking free
or caged,
held to this life, as if engraved in
granite.
held to this, as the first sunlight
comes through the blinds and as
your shoes wait for
you.
held to this, through the symphonies
and the traffic,
through the wash of the hours.
held to this, through the seasons
and the voices and the barking of
dogs.
held to this, held to this
as the airliners crash.
held to this, as you walk, as you
talk, as you sleep.
held to this, as the suicides drown,
as the nursing homes burn,
held to this, held to this, held to
this, as the cat plays with the death of the
mouse.
as we move through it or think about
it or don't think about it,
we're held to this,
as the sun freezes in our center,
as we kick, as we squirm, as we make small
choices or as they are made for
us,
we're held to this, held to this, held to
this,
held.

I meet a vegetarian

they had ten cent hot dog night
at the harness races.
biggest crowd of the
year.
those lines were 90 feet
long.
some of those people never saw a single
race or made a single
bet.
each was limited to
2 hot dogs per
person.

admission was $5
parking was $3.
they needed a car and some
gas to get
there.

the lines never shortened
all night.

I walked over and bought
a bag of
50¢ popcorn.
"don't you wish you had a
ten cent hot dog?"
I asked the
girl.

"I'm a vegetarian,"
she said.

"give me a little more
butter than
that," I said, "this is my only
meal of the night."

I got my bag

put a handful in my
mouth
then
turned and faced the
toteboard.

she laughed.

the Nile runs north

I walked into the men's crapper
at the racetrack
and I counted them:
there were twelve men
urinating in the south
trough.
nobody was using the
north.

wherever the masses go,
you go the other
way.

I used the trough to the
north.

then I got out of there
and that day I damn near
swept the entire
card.

I knew how to handicap
horses and
men.

observation put to action
is the essence
of art.

all god's children got trouble

this guy murdered his
mother-in-law

chopped her up
put her in a trunk

put the trunk in his car
took his car to a bridge

held up 5:15 traffic for four minutes
while they all sat and watched him

he got out the trunk
lifted and pushed it over the side

got in his car
and it wouldn't start

sat in his car and noticed that the
trunk wasn't sinking but floating

some guy with a kind smile and
N.J. license plates pushed him to the end of the bridge

he got out and stole a bicycle and
rode it to the edge of the water

jumped into the river
and swam to the trunk

and pushed and pushed and struggled and
tried to make it sink

gave up and swam back to shore
a good 3/4's of a mile of swimming

found his car and got in and it
started

drove away very fast and got a ticket
for speeding

the cop wrote a ticket and checked to see
if he had any outstanding warrants

there were
several

they took him in and
booked him

they booked him for attempted suicide
and speeding and for the stolen bicycle

and finally for
murder

next time you think you've got it tough
think of that poor bastard.

my 3 best friends

the first is just a bum.
he loves to ride the rails,
the freights.
he comes by and tells me
about the treasures he finds in
the L.A. dump and
about murders on the road
and about the eccentrics
and madmen who abound in
the brush and at the mission
and on skid row and on the road.

the second is very white
and he lives in the black
ghetto of East Los Angeles
raises vegetables and
chickens in his back-
yard
gets up at 6 a.m. every
morning to stand guard over his
chickens.
first he sets alarms near all
the nests and then he
starts mixing and drink-
ing margaritas.
by 4 p.m. he is drunk
goes to bed and
sleeps
for his day
is done.

the last one is in and out
of madhouses.
he stole a car the other
day and drove all the way to
Texas
finally ending up at the
Dallas–Fort Worth
airport

thinking that
Madonna was
going to meet him there and
take him on a honeymoon to
the South Sea Islands.

these are the 3 most brilliant
men that I know, their minds and conver-
sations are full of intelligence,
humor and vision.

why is it that the sane, the rich and the
successful always know
so much less than the mad or
the nearly mad?

my doctor

I walked into the waiting room.
it was full.
mostly old,
dying women.

I asked the reception-
ist:
"where the hell is he?"

"I don't know," she said.
"he hasn't phoned in or
anything.
these people have been
waiting for hours. do you
want to wait?"

I walked back out and down the
stairway,
got into my car and
drove to the
racetrack.

I parked, locked it,
went in
and saw him standing there with
a hot dog and a beer.

he saw me: "Henry, can I buy
you a
hot dog and a beer?"

"listen," I told him, "I was
at your office.
I had an appointment.
there were
eleven old, dying women
in your waiting room."

"Martha will give them new

appointments," he said.

I walked over to the grandstand,
sat down and
studied the *Racing Form*.

my doctor appeared with a
hot dog and a beer.
"for you," he said.

"thank you," I said.

"it gets depressing,"
he told me. "there's one
old woman, she's got
cancer of the ass.
anybody else would *die!*
she just won't die!
I don't know what to
do with her!"

"bill her extra," I said.

"Martha takes care of
that," he answered.
"who do you like in the
first race?"

"I favor the six,"
I told him.

"the nine should win
by a nose," he said.
"by the way, why did you
need to
see me?"

"cancer of the ass,"
I told him.

"you're a funny

man," he said. "you're
one of my favorite
patients."

"have you ever screwed
Martha?" I asked.

"of course," he answered.
"you like her?"

"except when she bills
me," I told him.

"I think it's going to be the nine
horse," he said.

"you already bet?"
I asked.

"sure," he said.

I got up to bet,
came back
just in time to
see them break
from the gate.
my six horse
stumbled
getting out.

anyhow, the nine
won by a nose.

my doctor got up
to cash his
ticket.

I tried to remember
what I had gone
to see him
about.

then he was back.
he handed me another
hot dog and beer.
then he sat
down.

and started talking
about what
a horrible woman
his wife was.

a certain pride here

I don't care to have my writing
praised too often:
it's dangerous for the writing and
for me.

writing is what one does,
it's like a spider spinning its
web.
you do what you have
to do.

yet, regarding praise, I sometimes
weaken,
say when they write me
from the prisons that they
like my stuff.
or I like it better yet
when they write me
from the madhouse that they
like my stuff.

the bit I liked best, though,
was when the
madam of a Nevada whorehouse
wrote me
that she *and* the girls
liked my stuff

and anytime
I was in the neighborhood
I could have all of it I wanted
for free.

that beats
any notice I might get
in the *N. Y. Times*

hands
down.

a screening

arrived for the 2nd screening.
some of the crowd from the first screening
were still in the lobby
huddled in groups,
directors, assistant directors, screenwriters,
actors, producers, critics, friends of somebody,
cameramen, so forth.

I was told by one, "It's good, really
good, you'll laugh your head off!"

I went in with my wife and we sat down.
she was lucky, she was able to laugh a few
times.

I found the whole thing entirely
derivative.
there was a touch of Woody Allen
and some Marx Brothers, even a
bit of Chaplin,
a touch of this and that,
some dancing, screaming, some good
old cussing,
some Americana and memories of Italy
mixed in with some bad and
obvious writing.
one of the actors had won an award
somewhere for his
performance
which was ordinary.
and I could feel the joke lines coming
before they landed.
but the audience was clapping and
laughing and having a good
time.

god, I thought, watching, either I'm
right or I'm crazy and there's something
wrong with me.

maybe I lack the ability to
allow something simple and good to enter
my consciousness.
well, whatever I am, the I that I am
thinks that this is crap.

the lady behind us was just about
tearing up her seat
bellowing with laughter.

then it was over.
we had the end seats one row from
the back
and were able to get out
quickly.

we were first in line down in parking
except for one fellow who was
actually running for his car.
he leaped in and roared off.
we were not far
behind.

it was a pleasant ride home.
the night was dark and clean, it
had just stopped
raining.
and Hollywood had a hell of a
way to go
before it would ever get
there.

fame

some want it, I don't want it, I
want to do whatever it is I do
and just do it.
I don't want to look into the
adulating eye,
shake the sweating
palm.
I think that whatever I do
is my business.
I do it because if I don't
I'm finished.
I'm selfish:
I do it for myself
to save what is left of
myself.
and when I am
approached as
hero or
half-god or
guru
I refuse to accept
that.
I don't want their
congratulations,
their worship,
their companionship.

I may have half-a-
million readers,
a million,
two million.
I don't care.
I write the word
how I have to
write it.

and, in the
beginning,
when there were no

readers
I wrote the word
as I needed to write the
word
and if all
the half-million,
the million,
the two million,
disappear
I will continue to
write the
word
as I always have.

the reader is an
afterthought,
the placenta,
an accident,
and any writer who
believes otherwise
is a bigger fool than
his
following.

thoughts on being 71

having worn life like a red
flower,
I have reached here,
sitting in slippers and shorts while
listening to
Ravel.
time for a good cigar.
I note the wedding ring on one of
my fingers as I light
up.

also,
it's better now, death is closer,
I no longer have to look for it,
no longer have to challenge
it, taunt it, play with it.
it's right here with me
like a pet cat or a wall
calendar.

I've had a good run.
I can toss it in without regret.

odd, though, I feel no different
than I did at 35 or 47 or 62:
I am only truly conscious of my
age when I look into a
mirror:
ridiculous
baleful eyes, grinning
stupid mouth.

it's nice, my friend, the
lightning flashes about
me,
I've washed up on the golden
shore.
everything here is miracle,
a hard miracle,

as was what
preceded
this.

but there's nothing worse than
some old guy
talking about what he
did.

well, yes, there is:
a bunch of old guys talking about
it.

I stay away from them.
and you stay away from me.

that space is all we'll ever really
need.
any of
us.

at the end of the day

a fat Mexican woman in front of me
lays down two dollars all in change:
quarters, dimes and nickels
and calls the wrong number.
as I walk up, bet twenty-win and call the
wrong number too.
a flash of light erupts in the sky followed
by distant thunder.
small drops of rain begin their work and as we
go out to watch the last race:
12 three-year-olds at a flat mile, non-winners
of two races.
they break in a spill of color and gamble
fight for position on the quick turn, then
enter the backstretch before the indifferent
mountains.
there's still a chance for everybody
except then the 6 horse snaps a
foreleg and
tosses a millionaire called Pincay to the
hard hard ground as
some of the Mexican poor groan for him
most don't care
and a few are secretly delighted.
as the track ambulance circles counter-
clockwise
the race unfolds unfolds
as 3 contenders straighten out for the
stretch drive.
the favorite gives way
falls back
as the 2nd favorite and a 26-to-one longshot
drive to the wire as one 8-legged creature
the last head bob in the photo belonging to
the longshot.
most tear up their tickets then and begin
the walk to the parking lot (and to whatever else is
left over for them) as
the hot drops of rain increase, then

turn cold.
we all hope that our automobiles
will still be safely there as
Pincay regains consciousness in the track
infirmary and asks, "what the hell
happened?"

huh

dead in my shoes, scooped empty,
this is the place I never wanted to
be,
twisting in this chair
wondering where it all went
and when.

you're just another old
boy
with faltering voice and inaccurate
memories.
Senior Citizen's lunch,
social security,
you're no longer considered a
danger
by them or by
you.
you find yourself reading the
obituary columns.
dry stuff when it occurs
to others.

but you were hell-bent when you
were young, right?
that's what they all say,
all the old
farts.
tiresome babble.

ah, it's just a bad night.
you dropped your vitamins at
the track, there by the water
fountain, just before the
2nd race.
then forgot them.

tomorrow night you'll be
sitting with a tall bottle of red wine,
smoking those bitter

Italian cigars
and listening to Sibelius.

it's all a matter of waiting it
out properly, in good humor and
form.
be patient, it will
happen
again.

meanwhile, a good night's
sleep will
do.

until

we've got to live with loss and
maybe play
with a bad
hand

and

we know all the while what the score is.
we take it standing like Hemingway
or we dismiss it like
Camus
but we know
we know.

this is the way it works and
we wind our clocks and we
wait for

midnight or the carnival
a hamburger sandwich or the
garbage man.

we live with it and we live with it until we

die.

short story

on this pleasant day
as our President speaks of his compassion for the poor
I lay 40-win on Big John in the 8th, he's 3-to-one
going against a 2-to-5 shot, Time to Explode, who's
dropping out of a Stakes Race but it was a router and
I figure Big John—a sprinter—can out-jackrabbit
him at 5 and ½ furlongs

which is what happens: he pays $8.20 and I get back
$164
and strangely then I find myself
remembering the time I was starving in Miami
trying to write short stories ...

one night taking the last of my money I bought a
loaf of bread and a jar of peanut butter and
taking them up to my room and opening the bread
I found it green stinking rotten.

I ate the peanut butter with my fingers
I didn't have a knife
I had intended to smear the stuff on the bread
with a bottle opener.

when I opened the bread and saw the green
rotting mold
I was too insane
demented
confused
to take it back.
I just stood in that room and watched my face and eyes
in the dresser mirror as I dug my fingers into the
peanut butter
glad to have that much
alone with the peeling wallpaper and
the dozens of rejected stories ...

I lose the 9th and drive back in knowing that
everything can return back to where it was

without much difficulty and
as our President speaks of his compassion for the
poor
I remember Big John in the 8th, turn on the radio,
luck onto Brahms, accept the grace of that,
yet also think again about
the rotten green bread and
all those short stories turned away,
thrown away—
some I fear were very bad and some I fear were
not—
in that time
when not even the poor felt compassion
for themselves

as much as I hate to use the "F" word

maybe it's just because
I was young then
that I can't find anybody now
as exciting as I once found
T. S. Eliot, Pound, D. H.
Lawrence, Céline, Fante,
Hem and Turgenev,
and all those others,
most of them still alive
when I first read them.

maybe it's because I've
lost that first thrill of
living my life that
nothing is as exciting anymore,
neither other writers nor the life.

maybe it's just because
I've been writing
too long
that I yearn again
for the old joy of
turning page after page
the words carrying me on
into
new areas of
risk and meaning.

now I'm just
an old dog
who drives his car
on the freeway
and takes out
the garbage.

being an old professional writer
possibly deadens the
pleasure of reading others.
or perhaps

the others are a threat
that one tries to keep
from one's consciousness?

most writers I know now
only praise safely
dead writers or writers who
are their friends or allies.
when I die I expect suddenly to become
much more popular with
other writers

and to those who are quick to praise me
then, I say it now: *fuck
you.*

competition

we live by the harbor now
and at night
the ships often blow their
foghorns.

she is a light sleeper.
she will leap up,
sitting straight up
in the bed.

"DAMN!"

"what is it? what is it?"

"I thought you farted!"

"not that time, dear..."

she is a good child;
living with me has
dysfunctioned her nerves.
(actually, I like to save my
farts
for the bathtub.
those grey bubbles waft up
a magic stench.)

farting is much like fucking:
you can't do it all the time
but when you do
there oftentimes comes a
feeling of pride
as if your artistry
the act itself
is a rare and precious
thing.

I fart more than I fuck
and I fart better than I

fuck
and I am pleased
to be mistaken
for a foghorn
in the middle of the
night.

raw

my poems are raw
like the guts of a catfish
cut open.

what matters is the best
way in or out—
which is sometimes fucking
sometimes madness
sometimes suicide,
anything
handy.

words are all right
as words
but never let them
get in the
way.

hardly Nirvana

look, I asked the waiter, don't you have
beer in a bottle?
no, he answered.
wait, I said, in a place as big as this
you mean you don't have bottled
beer?
not the brand you asked for,
he responded.
but you do have other brands in a
bottle?
oh yes, he said.
then bring me one, I asked.
what kind?
any kind.
do you want me to take back the
glass of beer? he asked.
I'll drink it, I told him.

he walked off to get my beer.
it was a cold December night.
I felt like punching somebody
out.

I watched a cruise ship slowly
navigate the harbor.
I drank my glass of beer.

the waiter was back with my
bottle of beer.

thanks much, I told
him.

so much for the freedom of
choice
in this last bastion of
freedom.

Sunday nights in San Pedro
aren't very
much.

garden talk

"the great blaze of noon," said
the horned frog.

"no, the great noon blaze," said
the snail.

"no, nothing's great," said the
finch, "everything's equal."

"no, nothing's equal," said the
dog, "the balance is in the
differences."

"anyhow, it's too hot," said
the gopher.

"compared to what?" asked the
horned frog.

"there's no 'what,'" said the
snail, "is *is* 'what' and
'what' is what *is.*"

"what's that?" asked the finch.

"that's what," said the dog.

"and that's that," said the
gopher
who then
crawled down into his
hole
to get away
from
all of them.

a computer now

I was the drunk
typer in hock
who used to hand-print his
work with a pen
most of it short stories
to send to *The Atlantic
Monthly,*
Harper's
and *The New Yorker.*
oh yes, and to
Story magazine.

I'm sure they thought
me mad
and I might have
been
but I sent out
3 to 5 stories a
week.
the editor of the
Atlantic answered once
and the editor of
Story a few times with
little notes of
encouragement
so I knew the work was
read.

now I have a computer
and it too has its
little stories
of breakdowns and
lost work.
also, I must often
carry
the computer back
to the repair shop.
"I'm here again,"
I tell them.

ever since one of my
cats sprayed
into the slot where one
inserts the
disks
things have not been
well.

I leave the computer
at the shop and go back
to the electric typewriter
but it's like trying to break
huge boulders with a
sledgehammer
but I go ahead
and hammer
and finally get a few
lines.

I even tried the manual
typewriter once and
couldn't work
it.

I'm back to the computer
now
writing this
but can't help thinking of
the days when I hand-
printed everything.
I got so that I could hand-
print faster than I could write
in longhand.
drinking and hand-printing,
hand-printing and
drinking
and putting the stuff into
envelopes.

I was mad, yes,
I was mad

but gloriously mad,
young, drinking the cheap
wine,
smoking rolled cigarettes
whose red hot ash
often dropped on my
undershirt
burning me out of my
trance.

I can't go back to that,
I have my Macintosh
but I'm glad I was there
like that
lucky enough and crazy
enough to fling it out to
the wind.

sometimes we are given
something extra by the
gods and don't know it
at the time.

I look back now,
I look back at that kid
and I'm glad it was
me,
the gods up there
laughing and urging me
on,
having such a god-damned
good time about it
all,
me in that small room,
running that pen across the paper,
no automobile, no woman,
no job, no food,
just wine and ink and
paper,
the door closed,
my mind running along the

edge of the ceiling,
along the edge of the
night sky,
I just didn't know any
better and I
did.

a day so flat you could roll marbles on it

counted 12 bottles of soy sauce on the shelf
behind the counter.
the waitress poured me more
coffee.
nice girl, not worried about being
good looking.
it was 2 in the afternoon and I was
between one place and
another,
caught between dumb errands,
dumb but necessary.
well, nothing is necessary.
I remembered once
leaving my hotel
early in the morning
and walking out
into the desert and walking and
walking
but something pulled me back:
fear and custom.
and when I got back to the hotel
my bus was gone.

the waitress poured me more
coffee.
I would not sleep that
night.
I ate the chicken sandwich
and asked for the
bill.

outside my car was waiting.
I got in and drove toward my
next
dumb errand.
many days, years,
lives are used up like
this.

I know, I thought, driving along,
I've got the blues, the old
fashioned
blues.

the streets and the automobiles
flowed past and all around
me
and I couldn't cry and I couldn't
sing and I
couldn't
laugh.

and I didn't even have a cigarette
to help kill myself

as I drove on to my next
errand.

lazy in San Pedro

quiet
sunbathing naked in your own backyard
a 70-year-old fool
stretched out and uncaring as
your white cat licks its bunghole
(its blue mad eyes half closed).
the old gal next door had to go
to the hospital last week
sunburned her ass somehow
cost her 8 hundred dollars.

you have big balls and
powerful legs.
a jay screeches its maledictions
from a Pacific Telephone wire high above
as the church bells ring.

quiet
bugs on the leaves engage in
intercourse.
tonight you will probably
get very drunk.
(you smashed the bathroom window
last week.)
(you still have a good right
hook.)

don't burn *your* ass.
turn over. yes, like that.
lay your head back on your arms
pretend that life is bearable while
the whores in the park downtown
eat apricots, and the typewriter
sits upstairs
alone.

it's slow tonight

well, here I sit
again
listening to the good old
songs
again,
feeling sorry,
the good
old-fashioned
sorry
where the tears
don't quite
arrive.
fine.
I listen some more.

the mind can
consume magical
amounts of
memory
as night folds
into further
night,
as another cigar
is lit,
how awful
maudlin it can
get
as old
songs follow
each
other,
faces are
remembered,
young faces,
like new slices of an
apple,
they are dead
now,
almost all of

them
dead
now.

the seeming
beautiful and
the seeming
brave,
gone.

sitting here
allowing my
better senses
to be diluted by
melancholy,
an old
man,
remembering
again,
looking all up and
down the imaginary bar
full of empty bar
stools,
thinking of that
kid with the wild
red
eyes
who sat there
pouring them
down and down
and down
again
to the point of
imbecility,
now remembering,
listening
again,
allowing the foolishness
to enter
again.
we are all

fools forever.
fooled
forever.
gladly.
now.

an answer to an eleventh grade student in Philadelphia

don't worry about my
poem:

later
there are going to be other
things
out there

much worse
than what
you read
of mine
in class.

the yellow pencil

I am sitting in the stands with a
two-day hangover;
last night was the worst:
white wine, red wine and
tequila.

I am out there because I have
evolved an astonishing
new theory on
how to beat the horses.

the money is secondary:
it's only used as a guide
to keep me on
the correct path.

I won $302
the day before
and I am $265 ahead
going into the sixth.

I am dizzy and
I can barely function
but the new theory
(formula K) proves itself
over and over:
M plus S plus C plus O
(each brought down to
relative power of
1/4): and then each time
the horse with the
lowest total is
the winner.

it is like discovering
the very secret
of life itself.
when your formula tells you
that a 2nd, 3rd or 4th

favorite
will beat the favorite
and when your figures
select only *one* horse,
it is a very curious
feeling,
and you yearn to apply
the same precise simplicity to
other areas of existence,
in the spiritual
rather than in the material
realm.

I have my figures ready for the
6th race
then look up
and see
there in the stands above
me
a fellow sitting upright.
his face is smooth and
bland.
his expression is set
exactly at zero.

he has a yellow pencil
he flips it over
once
into the air and
catches it with
one hand.

he does it
again

and again

with the same perfect
timing.

what is he

doing?

he just sits there
and continues to
repeat the
maneuver.

I begin to
count:
one two three
four five six ...

23, 24, 25, 26,
27 ...

his movements are
graceless,
he reminds me of a
factory robot.

this man is my
enemy.

45, 46, 47, 48 ...

his face has the
taut dead skin
of a stuffed
ape

and I am sitting
with my two-day
two-night
hangover,
watching.

53, 54, 55 ...

this will be my
life in hell: watching
men like that

forever
tossing and
catching pencils
with one
hand
in that same
unbroken
rhythm ...

I feel vertigo coming on
I feel a pressing
at the temples
as if I was going
mad.

I can't watch
any longer.

I get up and walk
away
as I think,

it will never
let go
it will follow you
wherever you
go, supermarkets,
bazaars, track
meets, it will
find you, maul you,
piss all over you, let
you know
that it has found you
again.
and there will be
nobody
you can talk to
about it.

I find the bar.

the barkeep seems a nice enough
fellow: little bright blue
eyes and a crisp white
shirt.

"double vodka 7,"
I tell him.

he nods and moves
off.

a high-yellow in a
see-through blouse
throws her
head back and
laughs about
something.

she's about three
feet
to the left
so
that's far
enough.

the barkeep comes
back with
my drink
asks me:
"how's it going?"

I wink and
slide
the money
toward
him.

a grounder to the shortstop

ten minutes left to get the word
down.
why not, I've punched many
time clocks.
haven't been getting enough
sleep.
next day I drive the freeways
just as swiftly
but more on edge
taking a dislike to the other
drivers.
poor way to start a damned
day.
I will get under the covers
before one a.m.
tonight.
seven minutes left to get the word
down.
suppose it were the last seven
minutes of my life,
what would I say?
nothing.
sure.
death was never the problem
anyhow.

bad music on the radio.
five minutes left.

hell, I'm going to stop four
minutes early.
I'm in control.

let the gods rattle somebody
else's Venetian
blinds.

good night.

don't sit under the apple tree with anybody else but me

to choose
wisely is half way
along the
road to
victory;
the other half is
conquered by
indifference.

on the one hand
you can say
anything
you want;
on the other hand
you don't
have to.

somehow
I've managed
to do
both.

so any
problem you have
with me
is
yours.

secret laughter

the lair of the hunted is
hidden in the last place
you'd ever look
and even if you find it
you won't believe
it's really there
in much the same way
as the average person
will not believe a great painting.

PHOTO: Michael Montfort

CHARLES BUKOWSKI is one of America's best-known contemporary writers of poetry and prose, and, many would claim, its most influential and imitated poet. He was born in Andernach, Germany, to an American soldier father and a German mother in 1920, and brought to the United States at the age of three. He was raised in Los Angeles and lived there for fifty years. He published his first story in 1944 when he was twenty-four and began writing poetry at the age of thirty-five. He died in San Pedro, California, on March 9, 1994, at the age of seventy-three, shortly after completing his last novel, *Pulp* (1994).

During his lifetime he published more than forty-five books of poetry and prose, including the novels *Post Office* (1971), *Factotum* (1975), *Women* (1978), *Ham on Rye* (1982), and *Hollywood* (1989). Among his most recent books are the posthumous editions of *What Matters Most Is How Well You Walk Through the Fire* (1999), *Open All Night: New Poems* (2000), *Beerspit Night and Cursing: The Correspondence of Charles Bukowski and Sheri Martinelli, 1960–1967* (2001), and *Night Torn Mad with Footsteps: New Poems* (2001).

All of his books have now been published in translation in more than a dozen languages and his worldwide popularity remains undiminished. In the years to come Ecco will publish additional volumes of previously uncollected poetry and letters.